RIO QUEBEC

SOO CANAL !

MARIE

MONTREAL ●

STRAITS OF MACKINAC BRIDGE

CORNWALL ●

HURON

Georgian
Bay

PRESCOTT ●

St. Lawrence River

OGDENSBURG ○

KINGSTON ●●●
○○○
○○○

TORONTO ●

LAKE ONTARIO

NEW YORK

● BUFFALO

St. Clair
River

LAKE ERIE

CLEVELAND ●

RIO

PENNSYLVANIA

SOO CANAL!

Sweetwater Seas

In the land of Hiawatha
Where the Mississippi rises
For his never-ending journey
To the Gulf of Mexico,
Where the Falls of Minnehaha
Echo still the carefree laughter
Of the living *Laughing Water*
When she loved so long ago,
Dwell the blue-robed, white-capped maidens,
Dwell the five great lakes, the daughters
Of the mighty Mississippi,
Father of Waters.

Where the thunder of Niagara
Splits the gorge from shore to shore,
Where the shadows of the wigwams
Haunt each river's sandy floor,
In the land of sky-blue water,
Minnesota, Manistee,
Michigan, Wisconsin, Tashmoo,
Mackinac, Sault Ste. Marie,
Dwell the blue-robed, white-capped maidens,
Dwell the five great lakes, the daughters
Of the mighty Mississippi,
Father of Waters.

Where the forest whispers stories
While the flowers all aglow
Listen to Algonquin legends
From the land of long ago,
Where the waves in watercolors
Paint the portrait of the sky
From the faintest blush of sunrise
Till the schools of stars swim by,
Dwell the blue-robed, white-capped maidens,
Dwell the five great lakes, the daughters
Of the mighty Mississippi,
Father of Waters.

W. R.

SOO CANAL!

by

WILLIAM RATIGAN

For Janet Martin, with
the best wishes of the author,
William Ratigan

WM. B. EERDMANS PUBLISHING COMPANY

Grand Rapids   1954   Michigan

For

ELEANOR,
PATSY and ANNE

Foreword

This book tells the epic of the construction of the Soo Canal a century ago. As an Engineer, its monumental scope has always fascinated me. In the century to come, the Electronic Age, it will probably play an even greater role in the destiny of our country and of the world at large.

—DOUGLAS MacARTHUR

Author's Preface

The primary purpose of SOO CANAL! is the entertainment of the reader. It was written as a love story and an historical romance. However, I also have done my best in this process to give the public a definitive book on one of the most important but least known examples of American free enterprise. As Stewart H. Holbrook pointed out in his *Iron Brew* (the Macmillan Company, New York, 1939):

"(The building of the original Soo Canal) has not to this day been given its rightful place among American historical events. It is passing strange that so few Americans know anything about this canal. They will travel far to brag of having seen the Suez and Panama Canals, yet right at home is a (canal) that has no peer, anywhere. The amount of cargo carried through the Suez is piddling compared to the burden that goes through the Soo. As for the famed Panama ditch, it carries about half as much as the Soo. And remember, the Soo Canal operates only seven months in the year. The canal at the Soo has played a bigger part in America's development than the Erie did. It was a big factor in making good steel cheap and in putting the United States away out front in steelmaking. The Soo Canal is the greatest gateway of commerce on earth. The Soo Canal can be a picture, too, one that will not readily be forgotten, with a score of big freighters, plated sheer white with ice and belching black smoke straight up toward the frosty sky, waiting their turn at the locks. It is a beautifully grim picture, mostly blacks and whites, with a dash of red, and it still cries aloud for an artist to paint it."

The Soo has been called the most important mile in the United States and the most important commercial canal on earth. In times of war and rumors of war, the Soo becomes infinitely precious because it connects the iron fields with steel mills and defense plants. Recent uranium discoveries in the Superior region have added immeasurable importance to the Soo in this atomic age.

Although much of the research on SOO CANAL! has followed original lines and in several cases has uncovered facts long buried or corrected mistakes long copied, I wish to take this opportunity of paying my respects to such eminent and readable Great Lakes historians as Grace Lee Nute, Dana Thomas Bowen, Milo M. Quaife, Walter Havighurst, Harlan Hatcher, Arthur Pound, Fred Landon, John Bartlow Martin, Angus Murdoch, Meridel Le Sueur, and, of course, Stewart H. Holbrook.

Thanks of a more personal nature are due to the late Chase S. Osborn, Michigan's unforgettable Governor and Iron Hunter, whose name stands alone in its inspirational associations with the Lake Superior region; Miss Cornelia Fairbanks, librarian of the Fairbanks Athenaeum, St. Johnsbury, Vermont, who furnished me with a file of letters from Charles Harvey to her grandfather Joseph; Jean Hulburd of *Country Gentleman* magazine, Philadephia, whose editorial assistance was invaluable; Gail Curtis of the Michigan State Library, Lansing, who promptly and graciously fulfilled every request for source material; Henry J. Barbour of Fairbanks, Morse & Co., whose information about pioneers in scale-making proved of real service; Joseph E. Bayliss of Richards Landing, Ontario, and Sault Ste. Marie, Michigan, who loaned me rare old clippings; and my wife, without whom the book could not have been written.

This work of fiction is based on facts so fabulous that the imaginative passages may seem more believable than the real events to the general reader. The Soo Canal stands as a monument of free enterprise in continuous performance under the democratic system. To cite only one example — A hundred years ago the Fairbanks Company had a large hand in the building of the canal. Today, on the eve of the Centennial, the Soo Canal is kept open to navigation longer than was ever dreamed possible, by the history-making Coast-Guard Ice-breaker *Mackinaw*, equipped for its winter-smashing duties with Fairbanks-Morse diesels and Niagara-power pumps.

From the *Harvey's Hammer* in this novel to the *Mackinaw's* ability to make a speed of more than four knots through ice more than four feet thick—here is the real but incredible Centennial Story of the Soo Canal: 1855-1955.

W. R.

The Dockside Press,
Number One Shipyard Row,
Charlevoix, Michigan.

Contents

Book IV

ONTARIO RIBBON

Book V

SUPERIOR PASSPORT

EPILOGUE

BOOK ONE

Huron Belle

Tell us now a tale of wonder,
Tell us of some strange adventure,
That the time may pass more gayly.

Song of Hiawatha

BOOK ONE

Huron Belle

1

TRAVELING SALESMAN STORY

PUTTING it one way, this is the century-old story of a traveling salesman who went to Sault Ste. Marie for a rest cure — and built the Soo Canal. Putting it another way, this is a love story — but the real breaker of hearts is the Queen of Lakes, iron-throned and copper-crowned Superior, who still rules her wilderness at the headwaters of civilization and dares any company of adventurers to come and take what she holds dear.

Putting it any way at all, Henry Wadsworth Longfellow rightfully opens and closes the story. To a dead-heat finish, willy-nilly, he raced an epic poem against an epoch-making canal, to share this much in common with the traveling salesman: they both produced enduring masterworks for generations yet to come, and they were prodded into action by the same force of nature, a young steamboat captain who was a Great Lakes booster from the word *go*.

2

MR. LONGFELLOW AT HOME

On a summer morning about a hundred years ago, Professor Longfellow of Harvard University returned from a stroll around Cambridge to find the mail set out for him in the garden. His thatched brows puzzled out the bulky package delivered by Harnden's Express: publishers were always sending him dull books to review. Then his eyes brightened on a letter from Buffalo by Capt. E. L. Ringgold.

15

Nothing dull ever blew from that quarter, as the first few lines indicated:

> ESTEEMED COUSIN: This has been an uneventful trip so far, but it shows signs of improving. Yesternight Patrick Flynn and his Jug of Rumbellion and myself met a crew of salt-water sailors who called our Great Lakes naught but puddles. Some heads, and Pat's jug, were broken, but we escaped the Riot Squad by swimming out to the *Huron Belle*. . . .

With a chuckle and shake of his head, Henry Wadsworth Longfellow stopped reading to recall other escapades of the whim-whamsical scamp who had first introduced himself as Eureka Longfellow Ringgold in a letter from Vera Cruz. The letter claimed kinship through a Pennsylvania branch of the family and went on to recite, with modest flourishes, the capture of Santa Anna's wooden leg at the Battle of Cerro Gordo.

Letter after letter had continued the saga of Cousin Ringgold. He returned from the Mexican War to dash off a song for Christy's Minstrels before joining the stampede to California in a Cleveland barkentine. It was Ringgold who charted the course — out Lake Erie by way of the Welland Locks, across Lake Ontario and down the St. Lawrence River canals to the Atlantic, then around the Roaring Horn and through the Golden Gate — to show how the Great Lakes could be connected with the Seven Seas, and to make sailing history and his own fortune in one voyage. Home again, he had bought the steamboat of his dreams and began to promenade her from Sackets Harbor to the Soo, from toe to tip of navigation, singing the praises of his beloved sweet-water seas and of the blue-ribbon rivers that tied them together.

Professor Longfellow heaved a sigh, a wistful middle-aged sigh, in envy of his swashbuckling young relative. Cousin Ringgold sounded fabulous, even to his name. Why should any parents christen their son Eureka? Where, to raise a stranger question, had this Pennsylvania branch of the family originated? They were nobodies! Feeling vaguely comforted, Professor Longfellow resumed his reading of the letter:

> Forgive me another sermon, Coz, but this is Moving Day in the Nation and the compass points toward North Star, Setting Sun, and Lake Superior. The password is: 'Hustle up, slowpoke, you're obstructing progress, we got business with white pine and red iron ore, coin copper and Glasgow Bonnet wheat, Mackinaw trout and Fond du Lac furs, we got to plant cities like we plant corn and we should have harvested the crop yesterday, so pass us through, bub, stand aside for the future, here comes Manifest Destiny rampaging for the Roof of the World and the Greatest Lake on the Map, don't get killed in the rush, brother, Gangway for Tomorrow!' That's the password, Coz — Gangway! End of Sermon, but by this same post I send you the collected works of Henry Rowe Schoolcraft and I trust that the raw history on his pages may jolt you from your New England rut and inspire your Muse to recognize realms beyond Boston and halls west of Harvard. Very seriously, Coz, a poem by Longfellow on the Lake Superior country would be worth a thousand Horace Greeley editorials. My address for the next thirty days will be Sault Ste. Marie, Michigan. Hoping to hear from you soon, I remain, honored cousin, your most humble admirer and obedient servant,

> *Captain Eureka Longfellow Ringgold*

Professor Longfellow put down the letter and smiled thinly. Of course, ha-ha-hum, he took the jibe about New England in good grace but — did Cousin Ringgold think poems were written on order, with delivery guaranteed in thirty days? Not that there need be any real difficulty about that, but it was the principle of the thing. Besides, these Schoolcraft books were probably duller than the usual brand. Well, nothing to do but unwrap the package and find out the worst.

It was two hours later when Mrs. Longfellow called her husband to lunch. First she called from the kitchen window, then from the garden gate, and finally she stole up behind him and snatched a book from under his nose. Then she kissed him back to Cambridge, without scolding, because she had been wife to a poet long enough to realize that Henry must have been a thousand miles away when she called.

Hugging him from behind, her arms warm and soft around his neck, she caught a glimpse of boldly penned instructions on a remnant of wrapping paper: "If this package cannot be delivered to Professor Longfellow, proper payment is assured for its safe return to Captain Ringgold, aboard steamer *Huron Belle,* care of the Great Lakes."

"The charming impudence of the young scamp!" she smiled. "Who but that magic-carpet cousin of yours would dream of using the world's mightiest inland waterway as a personal forwarding address?" She began to tug her husband toward the house. "Why, at this very minute, he could be carrying his calling card to any one of five lakes larger than most seas, to a thousand ports located along both sides of an international boundary line. And yet, 'Address me, care of the Great Lakes,' says Cousin Ringgold grandly. There speaks a Longfellow to the spit-and-image, sirrah, vain as peacocks every one of you, but"—with mock severity—"there'll be one less of you unless a certain Henry W. marches straightway into the house for his lunch!"

3

THREE DAYS UP FROM BUFFALO

While Mrs. Longfellow teased her husband about his cousin's geographically haphazard forwarding address, the *Huron Belle,* three days up from Buffalo and pretty as a slice of wedding cake on a blue platter, side-wheeled a bend in the St. Mary's River to gain sight of Sault Ste. Marie in the sun-sparkled distance. As passengers rushed to the rail, Captain Ringgold poked a megaphone out the wheel-house.

"Approaching the head of navigation on the Inland Seas!" he warned. "We dock in five minutes, so get ready to change ship for the mining fields!"

There were two privileged passengers inside the wheel-house. Ringgold always showed special favors to the prettiest girl aboard, and on this trip Genesee Trowbridge defied competition. She had hair like young cornsilk, a complexion to eat with a spoon, and a way of promenading the deck that was a spring tonic. Her only drawback, in Ringgold's eyes, was the father she insisted on never letting out of her sight. Daniel Trowbridge was a middle-aged widower shrunk inside his skin by the respiratory trouble that had forced him to sell out a prosperous business in New York and go in search of a crisper climate. His lack-luster glances moved tiredly from white-capped river to pine-stippled shore, and he leaned gratefully on his daughter's arm. Genesee, bright and vital in contrast, had the typical woman's question to ask Ringgold.

"Why do we have to fuss and bother about changing boats? Why can't we stay on yours all the way up into Lake Superior?"

He admired the green parasol that protected her loveliness. "Because," he explained patiently, "we're coming into the Soo bottleneck where the greatest body of fresh water in the world blows its cork and champagnes over St. Mary's Falls. Not even the *Huron Belle* can buck Lake Superior when it comes boiling and busting out like that and blocks passage to the Iron Mountains and the Copper Country. I have to dock her below the rapids just like any common ordinary teakettle on a raft, and send my passengers hopping to the other dock about a mile above the rapids."

Daniel Trowbridge tightened the shawl around his thin shoulders. "Will we have any trouble getting transportation to the mines?"

"Don't worry about that," Ringgold assured him. "If there's nothing bound for Lake Superior this afternoon, there'll be a steamer out first thing in the morning." He hesitated because he generally rebelled at good advice himself, then took the plunge. "I wish you'd give up the idea of going up there, sir. Boom diggings and tent towns are no place for a man who's poor in health and rich in a good-looking daughter."

To cover his own embarrassment, Ringgold poked the megaphone out the wheelhouse again. "Fort Brady on the American side, Hudson Bay Post on the Canadian!" he bawled. "And the Falls of St. Mary's dead ahead!"

He felt Genesee Trowbridge tugging at his sleeve. She pointed excitedly toward a colonial mansion, frontier model, with its grove of umbrella elms and its wide lawn sloping to the river. Her lips shaped a question.

"That's Elmwood," he replied. "The Government used it for an Indian Agency, but it's vacant now. Formerly the residence of Henry Rowe Schoolcraft——"

He intended to tell her much more about Schoolcraft in hero-worshipping style, but Genesee had turned to her father. "Look, darling! The place was just made for us! Oh, if only we could live there, instead of renting some horrible shack in an out-of-the-way mining town!"

Momentarily, Daniel Trowbridge caught some of her enthusiasm. Like his daughter he could appreciate the social and business advantages in an estate that commanded the approaches to Sault Ste. Marie, where the whole world had to go by the front door en route to Lake Superior.

"If that isn't just like a woman, wanting to set up housekeeping before we get off the boat!" he said, with a chuckle that ended in a cough. "First thing I've got to do is find a good proposition to invest our money in——"

"Don't worry, darling, you'll find one." Love and pity trembled on the lips that brushed her father's sallow cheek.

"And the air is balsam and wine. I know this country will cure you."

As the two moved away, Ringgold watched the exciting mystery of Genesee's walk and tried to convince himself that he had been entirely unselfish in urging Trowbridge to stay away from Lake Superior's mining camps.

4

REPRESENTING FAIRBANKS SCALES

The *Huron Belle* swept upstream past Elmwood toward the foam and roar of the rapids. Captain Ringgold began to ease the helm around. The tail of his eye caught glimpses of the deck below, where impatient prospectors in homespun and would-be mining kings in broadcloth jammed the rails.

Boots pounded up the companionway. "Look at them down there, restless as caged animals," commented Charles T. Harvey, stepping briskly into the wheelhouse. "Sleek city cats and lean territorial wolves, ready to pounce on virgin wilderness."

Ringgold nodded to the fair-haired, broad-shouldered Yankee who had kept the trip alive with questions. "Most of them will go home broke, those that don't leave their bones to polish wild teeth, but a few will sail their hats into the air, start digging where the hats fall, and turn up the richest claims in creation."

"Too much of a gamble to suit me," Harvey said. "I'll stick to selling Fairbanks Scales."

"Ambition weighed and found wanting!" scoffed Ringgold. "You'd better keep a close lookout for opportunity, mister. In this country, it not only knocks, but it knocks you down and steps on you if you aren't careful!" He grinned, spinning the helm. "Ready to dock. Now maybe you'll stop asking questions."

"When a man stops asking questions," said Charles T. Harvey without a smile, "he might as well dig a hole and bury himself."

"I'll buy that, brother," said Ringgold. On the haul up from Buffalo, the two had found themselves well matched in many ways. They were large and rugged men in their early twenties with the drive and thrust that was spurring a seaboard nation across a continent to another coast. Brimming with ideas and energy, they made a well-balanced pair.

Connecticut-born Harvey was a traveling salesman sent by his Vermont firm to the healthful Lake Superior region to speed up recovery from a typhoid-fever attack. He had seen peculiar sights on the trip, but now, as the *Huron Belle* approached shore, his eyes almost popped out of his head at the spectacle of a large schooner moving overland toward Lake Superior, her masts and spars rising between houses, her bowsprit pointed up a business street, her majestic bulk by-passed by a bustle of carts and wagons.

Captain Ringgold laughed and explained how a cradle had been built for the vessel and how she was inched around the portage on greased ways with the aid of capstans. "Takes anywhere from one to three months," he said. "In the winter, I've seen them shoved across on sleds, but it's murderous slow work any time of year. That's why there are fewer ships on Superior than I've got fingers." His fist took a bear-cub swipe at Harvey's biceps. "And don't give me that Yankee stare and ask why we haven't built a canal. We've tried, some of us, but——" He shrugged his disdain of excuses, then jangled the engine room.

5

Wings on her Feet

Down below, Patrick Flynn, engineer, lowered a jug of Rumbellion to the crook of his elbow, directed a spray of Crabapple Cut Plug at a squeak in the machinery and ordered his firemen to remove the ponderous heads of Algoma cheese that had been holding down the safety valve. With her boilers free to breathe, the *Huron Belle* let off steam and blew for a landing.

In answer to the whistle came the peal of the Baptist Mission bell ashore. Through his glass, Ringgold spotted a young girl tugging at the hand rope. She had red hair bows to anchor her Indian braids and she was laughing for sheer joy of life. A moment later she sped down Water Street toward the dock to share the eternal excitement of a ship coming in. Ringgold understood the thrill that put wings on her feet. *Who knows what a ship may bring?* So she ran with her skirts hiked up, with golden legs aglint in a froth of petticoats, and Ringgold's lips curved as he saw how scandalized were the sour old coal-skuttle bonnets in her path.

"Is that bouncing little savage a friend of yours?" asked Harvey.

"Never saw here before, but that's the kind I'd pick for a kid sister," said Ringgold, then barked orders through his megaphone.

Bells jangled, paddle wheels churned in reverse; the *Huron Belle* bumped the docks, lines snaked out and snubbed her fast. Up from below lumbered Patrick Flynn, with flaming hair and a peat-smoke brogue. He heaved out the gangplank and roared: "Last one off is a carrot-nosed son of King William of Orange, but ladies first, ye spalpeens, or I'll teach you manners with my maulies!" And he brandished a pair of fists that were red-fuzzed rocks.

A party of sight-seeing schoolmarms surged ashore toward the whitewashed blockhouses of old Fort Brady, but the men all turned up in the opposite direction where a trapline of grogshops and bowling alleys staggered up a mud-crusted street that passed for civilization in the backwoods. At the end of the dock most of the newcomers stopped to stare at the gaudy banners that proclaimed:

PUBLIC AUCTION!

Why Hunt Copper and Iron in Lake Superior?
There Is a Gold Mine Right Here at the Soo!
Your Bid May Make Your Fortune Today!

6

TWO AUCTION ESCORTS

In 1852 Sault Ste. Marie—described by Henry Clay in an anti-canal speech as the "remotest settlement in the United States, if not the moon"—could boast of being the third oldest community under the American flag, but it had remained a fish-and-fur outpost on a paddle-and-portage route until the recent discoveries of copper and iron in the Lake Superior country westward. Now the Soo was busting its britches to hustle the multiplying trade and traffic around the rapids. These were flush times, the Soo was a boom town; men with jingle in their jeans and stars in their eyes were willing to bet on anything.

Even Daniel Trowbridge forgot an ailing man's pessimism as he studied the auction banners and remembered Captain Ringgold's advice. He had lingered on deck to avoid the rush of disembarkation. Beside him, his daughter Genesee twirled her green parasol and looked back over her shoulder at Captain Ringgold and Charles Harvey with the faintest trace of pique twinging her brows. All the way from Buffalo the one, in traditional sailor style, had courted and complimented and kept roses in her cheeks, but the traveling salesman had made not the slightest romantic overture.

With the intellectual honesty that was basic in her nature, Genesee recognized the feminine perversity that ruled her emotions. "I'm attracted to him," she said under her breath, "because he's handsome and well-bred and very masculine— and because he's the *only* man who has *ignored* me!"

Her thoughts were disrupted by pandemonium on land.
Several shots tore holes in the peaceful sky. A horse reared
in its traces, then bolted for the woods. An Ottawa squaw
with a papoose cradled on her back shrieked and dived
through the skin door of a wigwam. Almost everyone else
within hearing stampeded *toward* the sound of danger.

Quick steps drummed the deck and Genesee turned as a
large hand swallowed her elbow. "Two escorts volunteering to
show you the excitement," said Ringgold, and, glancing
from his to Harvey's face, Genesee noticed the essential difference between the young men—Ringgold's dancing eyes,
quirked mouth, and weather-bronzed recklessness in contrast
to Harvey's calculating scrutiny, determined lips, and Yankee
caution. Swashbuckling romanticist—and sober realist; a
team to make headlines in history. But all she saw was a
steamboat skipper and a traveling salesman, with their beards
and their reputations still to grow.

"Your daughter will be safe with us," Harvey assured Trowbridge.

"Bet your life," seconded Ringgold.

More shots rang out as Genesee let herself be hustled over
the gangplank, up the wharf, and toward a spile-legged warehouse that seemed the focal point of commotion. With broad
shoulders and ready elbows, Harvey and Ringgold cleared a
path through the crowd for her and her father until she had
a tiptoe view of a fat man standing on a freight wagon, with
the smoke still curling from one of Samuel Colt's new Patent
Pacifiers that lay on a barrel in front of him.

"Well, look at fat Philo Worts make a show of himself to
drum up an auction!" said Ringgold. "Worts owns the Soo
Portage Company," he explained to the others. "Mighty
shrewd trader in his business deals, with a nose for money
like a shark for blood. Listen to him spiel!"

7

GENESEE BIDS HIGH

"Starting off with a bang!" announced the fat man identified as Philo Worts. "What's all the shooting about? Draw closer, friends." He pounded the barrelhead with the Colt. "Hear that? It's opportunity knocking. Draw a little closer, friends."

And then from Philo's lips these new-come prospectors and capitalists from below heard that there was no need for at least one shrewd investor among them to brave the tent life and rough fare of the mining camps. Some lucky somebody could stay right here and make money, hand over fist. How? Draw closer, friends.

Forced as much by her own curiosity as by the pressure of the crowd behind her, Genesee squeezed nearer to hear the fat man's explanation.

All merchandise, machinery, and supplies for the Lake Superior ports had to be unloaded below the Falls of St. Mary's, carted around the rapids on horsecars, and put aboard another ship. What's more, every ton of iron blooms, every pound of pure copper from Lake Superior's mines had to be unloaded above the Falls of St. Mary's, carted around the rapids on the same horsecars, and put aboard a different ship. So, who got the business coming and going? The portage companies!

They could see the strap-iron railroad of the Chippewa Portage Company as it curved up the main street. The rival Soo Portage Company had a new pine wharf and a plank road along the portage. These two outfits controlled the trade —upwards of a hundred thousand barrels a year at twelve and one-half cents a barrel. Could a man hope to find a sounder investment?

Fat Philo Worts banged the Colt on the barrel. "Draw closer, friends. I need cash and I'll sell myself short to get it. I'm auctioning off the Soo Portage Company—plank road, pine wharf, four freight wagons, eight horses, two mules. What am I bid? Make me an offer, make yourself rich!"

As if he had been holding his breath, Ringgold exploded air. "Selling out at auction!" His face mapping surprise, he shook his head thoughtfully at the others. "Worts must need money bad. There's nothing better than the portage business around here—except, of course, striking it rich in the mine fields."

As the bids came in, shouted by men who hailed from Boston, Philadelphia, Indianapolis, Baltimore, from whistle stops, four corners, steamer landings,—Ringgold pointed out the pattern of the auction to Harvey and the Trowbridges. "Looks like Fat Philo has hired Cole Slater to see that the bidding goes high enough to suit him. Notice how Slater—he's the big black-whiskered gent next to the girl with the Indian braids—notice how he boosts the bid one dollar each time. He's general manager of the Soo Portage, but he hasn't got the kind of money he's talking."

Genesee's eyes were shining and her lips were parted breathlessly, but Daniel Trowbridge shook his head dubiously. "I don't understand this method of doing business," he told Harvey. "A large investment is involved here, and most of these men have just stepped off a boat. How can they possibly think of bidding so much without investigating--?"

"You're on the frontier," Ringgold said. "Up in this neck of the woods, greased lightning's a mud turtle compared with how a man's got to move if he wants to get anywhere ahead of the stampede. Worts timed this auction to meet the *Huron Belle's* passengers because he knows the temper of these copper and iron hunters. They aren't afraid of risking mere dollars on a sure-fire business deal."

Genesee's eyes were thoughtful. "Is it really a safe investment?"

"Safe?" Ringgold laughed shortly. "Everyone knows that hauling stuff around the rapids is the best-paying proposition at the Soo."

Daniel Trowbridge pursed his lips. "Are you quite serious?"

"Yes, sir. You might say that the portage business *is* the Soo."

"If it's such a profitable enterprise," Harvey broke in quietly, "then why is this fellow selling out?"

"Can't say for sure," Ringgold shrugged. "Philo Worts is a speculator. He always has his hands in half a dozen pies. Maybe he needs fast money for a big mining deal—"

"I wonder—" Genesee began. A wistful expression touched her face and she half-turned toward her father. They exchanged brief but significant glances. A moment later their heads bent together in whispered consultation. He asked a final question and she nodded. Yes, for his sake it would be better to invest their money here rather than risk the hardships and uncertainties of Lake Superior's boom towns. Now to save his lungs, she called out: "Mr. Trowbridge bids twenty-five hundred dollars."

Necks were craned toward the green parasol. Genesee held her head high. More than auction fever glowed in her cheeks. *I like to be looked at by men,* she admitted to herself. *Does that make me different?*

Ringgold whistled. "Nothing slow about the Trowbridges!" he said in a voice meant to be overheard.

"You said it would be a good idea for us to stay here at the Soo," Genesee reminded him. Her smile had saucy highlights. "This is the frontier, Captain, and we can't afford to be mud turtles — Twenty-seven hundred and thirty dollars!" she called, topping the last bid.

"And a dollar more!" roared black-whiskered Cole Slater.

By tens, by hundreds, by Slater's monotonous "And a dollar more," the bidding soared. At the forty-five hundred mark, only Cole Slater opposed Genesee. A warning headshake from her father served notice that they were near their limit. She turned to Ringgold for advice. Would five thousand be a fair price?"

"Dirt cheap. But Worts won't let the portage business go for that. He'd signal Slater to jump the bid."

"That, sir, remains to be seen." With characteristic impulsiveness Genesee staked everything on one last play:

"Five thousand dollars! And that's our final bid!"

Colt handle rapped the barrelhead. "Sold!" barked Philo Worts. "Step up and bind the bargain!"

8

Fist Fight

Pride of ownership staining his pallid cheeks, Daniel Trowbridge tugged at his money belt as he moved forward. Genesee, flushed with triumph, swept along on his arm. Harvey shouted at them, "Congratulations!" and then, spotting the puzzled frown that Ringgold wore, asked him: "Anything wrong?"

"I wish I knew." Ringgold scowled as twenty-dollar gold pieces spilled from Trowbridge's money belt onto Wort's barrelhead. "I'm not the kind to look for holes in doughnuts, but I feel responsible for advising the Trowbridges to jump at an investment here, and I don't like the sudden way Worts snapped up that low bid."

"You suggested he might need hard cash for another quick deal."

"Sure, sure, but I'd feel better if they had good legal advice, and I've meddled enough." Ringgold grasped Harvey's arm and pointed out a thin, white-haired gentleman inspect-

ing Indian handiwork in front of a waterside wigwam.
There's Judge Saltonstall. You played chess with him on the
Huron Belle. Would you ask him to check the bill of sale
and the deed to the property?"

"Good idea," said Harvey, and started off. Ringgold lost
sight of him in the surging mass of buckskin and broadcloth.
Amid the confusion that anticlimaxed the auction, a sound of
scuffling and a girl's half-smothered yelp attracted Ringgold's
attention. He shot across space toward a tangle of black whiskers and red hairbows.

"Slater! Take your paws off that girl!"

Ringgold's hand tore half the shirt from Slater's back as he
wrenched him around. Slater's eyes were ugly and he started
to bring his fists into play.

Lunging inside the wild swing, Ringgold smashed Slater
amidships and, as the hulking portage manager sagged forward, clubbed him across the back of the neck with a fist that
pile-drove him into the dirt. Trying to shake the stars from his
skull, Slater struggled to his feet. Too dazed to think straight,
he spoke thickly:

"What's the fuss about, sailor? Can't you tell she's only a
breed?"

This time Ringgold hit him even harder, screwing his
knuckles ruthlessly into the brutal mouth. Slater reeled back-
ward, tumbled over a sawhorse and sprawled inert, his
smashed lips grinning with pain.

Men came to look but they spoke softly and they gave wide
berth to Ringgold. He asked the girl if she had escaped
harm. She nodded pertly.

"I would have bitten off his nose in another minute, and
done much execution with my knee. However, thank you,
Captain Ringgold. I am called Susan Marie Beaufait Eldridge Johnston."

He guessed her age at no more than fifteen. Her voice was
musical, with the most curious blend of French and British

accents. So, she belonged to the famous Johnston clan. Strange, he had never seen her before.

She sensed the reason for his puckered brows and came to the rescue in a helter-skelter of explanation. "I have been just this past month dismissed from Sacred Heart Convent in Quebec, and now I am home for good, because the Holy Sisters said I would never be anything but a poor excuse for a nun, so I am sorry for the years they have wasted trying to teach me, but can I help it if there is an imp in my heart that makes me do wicked things like putting salt in Sister Grace Electa's tea and a bullfrog in the Mother Superior's closet?"

"Of course not," said Ringgold, choking down the laughter to maintain a straight face. "You can't be held responsible for what an imp does."

"*Vous avez raison,*" agreed Susan Marie gravely, with a momentary lapse into French. "One inherits such an imp the way one inherits a family nose, and surely one can't be blamed for *that.* You see," she went on swiftly, "my grandfather was one very black sheep, and—but that is another long story and I am supposed to be home to peel the potatoes. Me, I am very much like my grandfather!"

Her curtsy swept the ground. For a second he was held by the spell of her eyes that were like rainbows struck by lightning. Then she broke the spell by wrinkling her nose and darting out a pink tongue to mock her grande dame manners. The next moment she was away down the street in a puff of petticoats, and out of sight. But Ringgold never forgot that first discovery of her eyes.

9

HIS TRUE LOVE

Several minutes later, self-conscious of the frilly handkerchief that Genesee had insisted upon knotting around his bruised knuckles, Ringgold volunteered to show Harvey and

the Trowbridges the sights of the Soo as they started up Water
Street in search of lodgings. His spirits were high for three
reasons: he still tingled from the fight, he was strolling with a
beautiful girl, and Judge Saltonstall had pronounced Worts'
papers in order.

Genesee, glancing back over her shoulder at the spectacle of
Slater restored to his senses and clutching at a proffered
bottle, made a grimace of disgust and said, "The man's nothing but a wild animal!"

Ringgold laughed. "That's the kind who survive in this
country. Slater's as tough as they come, but he fits his job.
You can't hire a mollycoddle to boss a gang of roughnecks."

For an eloquent instant Genesee allowed her eyes to linger
on Ringgold's throbbing knuckles before she inquired demure-
ly, "Do you always put in a kind word for someone you've
just"—she hunted an apt phrase—"mopped the dirt with?"

"I never carry a fight beyond the knockout," said Ringgold.
"Life's too full of important things to leave room for grudges."
His devil-may-care grin invited her to share his philosophy.
"A man's like a melon. You can always get a pretty fair idea
what's inside by giving him a good thumping."

Daniel Trowbridge had been an interested listener to the
by-play. "Then you wouldn't advise us to employ a different
general manager."

"Why make trouble for yourself just because I took exception to the cut of his jib?" retorted Ringgold. "Slater's
no parlor pet, but he'll be a handy tool if you keep him nailed
down in place—and his place is bullwhacking that bunch of
dock-wallopers and mule skinners you inherited from Worts."

"Can I trust him?" asked Trowbridge.

"Sure. As long as you pay him more than he can steal
from you."

Harvey chuckled. "In other words, Slater is no worse than
most!"

With the gentlest pressure on Ringgold's arm, Genesee ended the discussion. "I thought, sir, you were going to acquaint us with the Soo?"

He pointed out the simple geography of this Great Lakes crossroads. Eastward, Water Street extended to Fort Brady below the rapids, where sailboats and steamboats from the Lower Lakes thrust their masts and stacks against the sky. Out in the boil of white water bobbed birchbark canoes in which Ojibways with the poise of tightrope walkers balanced their long-poled dipnets to catch whitefish. Farther downriver the windows of Elmwood reflected the setting sun.

Looking westward along Water Street the masts and stacks of Lake Superior's shipping could be seen, hardly half a mile away above the rapids. Right in the bottleneck between the two anchorages, the village of the Soo—perhaps a score of business houses and a hundred dwellings—sprawled on the riverbank facing the Falls of St. Mary's and stared across at the Canadian shore where the Hudson's Bay Post dominated a few shacks and wigwams.

"Not much different than most frontier towns," Ringgold admitted to Genesee. "About a dozen grogshops to every real home."

"Are you for Temperance?" asked Harvey, genuinely interested.

Ringgold took a side glance at Genesee before replying. "Whisky is a bad thing," he said piously, "especially bad whisky."

They had been following the portage railroad tracks up the middle of the street. Suddenly a rumbling shook the ground and they all scrambled for safety as a team of mules, tongue-lashed by a Canuck driver, whirled its tramcar over the rails toward the docks below the rapids.

"Lake Superior copper and iron, bound down for Cleveland and Pittsburgh," announced Ringgold. "There's your portage business in operation, Mr. Trowbridge."

"I'm more interested in getting accommodations right now than in anything else," he said tiredly. "Would you recommend this Hotel Chippewa?"

A drunken lumberjack lurched out of the sagging building chased by a screeching chambermaid. Ringgold hastily steered his party across the street. Two doors beyond the office of the *Soo Sentinel,* he led them into the cool lobby of the Soo's other hotel, the Van Anden House, where the clerk assured Daniel Trowbridge of the best rooms north of Detroit.

Harvey began to shake hands and make his adieus. "But I thought——" Genesee began in pretty confusion. "Aren't you going to stay here too?"

"No, I think a boarding house will fit my pocketbook better."

"We'll be seeing you, won't we?"

"You'll be seeing *me!*" Ringgold promised. Outside again, he showed Harvey to the gate of a pleasant two-story yellow house and told him to inquire for Mrs. Bingham, wife of the Baptist minister, who took in guests.

Harvey stared up at the bell on the roof. "Why, that must be the bell the little savage was ringing before she dashed down to the dock——"

Ringgold nodded. "But don't let her hear you call her a savage. She's Irish Indian, and they don't come any wilder than that combination. If I'd known she was a Johnston, I might have stayed clear of the fight, and let Slater take his medicine." He chuckled, turned away and called, "Well, so long, take it easy."

"Where are *you* going to stay?"

"With my sweetheart." Catching Harvey's expression, Ringgold laughed and added, "Aboard the *Huron Belle,* you ninny, she's my true love."

10

SALESMAN: TO SELL THE FUTURE

During the following week the Trowbridge Portage Company began business, and Genesee Trowbridge received nine proposals of marriage, including two from Captain Ringgold, but she would have traded them all for a good word from Charles Harvey, who soaked up sun on the front porch of Mrs. Bingham's boarding house until Saturday, when things began to happen.

That was the day the historic *Illinois,* Captain Jack Wilson, master, steamed up to the Soo. Wilson hailed Ringgold and tossed a *Detroit Free Press* to the dock. "Finally got the go-ahead," he bellowed. "Now we need a go-getter with jingle in his jeans and miracles to pull out of his beaver."

Ringgold needed only one look at the paper.

**GOVERNMENT OFFERS LAND GRANT —
HOPES FOR SOO CANAL REKINDLED**

The headlines told him why Worts had sold out of the portage business for a fast song. The pork-jowled speculator must have had a political tip. Stuffing the *Free Press* in his pocket, Ringgold strolled up Water Street. Excitement churned within him, but he built up no high hopes. Wilson was right. They needed a man who could produce miracles.

Getting right down to essentials, they needed a salesman, a wizard who could sell ice to Eskimos—or even a canal on the moon to a state legislature. Ringgold knew only one salesman, and he lengthened his strides toward Mrs. Bingham's front porch where he flabbergasted a drowsy vacationist with his opening salvo.

"Listen, mister," he told Harvey, "this is a sky's-the-limit, nothing's-impossible nation with the same message for everybody. 'Step up and take what you want; if you don't see it, ask for it; if we haven't got it, we'll invent it.' " He smacked the porch railing with his fist. "Am I right?"

"No argument," agreed Harvey, eyes dazed and slightly bulged. "Here, take a seat in the shade."

"I'm not sunstruck!" snapped Ringgold. "Could you sell more than scales?" he demanded. "Could you sell faith in the future?"

"Faith in the future?" echoed Harvey. "That's what put Fairbanks Scales on the map. That's the chief stock in trade of every good salesman!"

"Then you're my hole card and I'm betting blind," said Ringgold, hauling him down to the portage where they could watch the pine-whiskered islands and black-shouldered rocks in the rapids and listen to the music of St. Mary's Falls. There he handed the salesman the *Detroit Free Press.*

The print jumped off the paper and darkened Harvey's eyes. Congress had approved, "An Act granting to the State of Michigan the right of way, and a donation of public lands for the construction of a ship canal around the Falls of St. Mary's in said state."

The situation amounted to this: Michigan had no money to spare for such a risky business, but there were 750,000 acres of land waiting for private enterprise as payment for construction of a ditch to link Lake Superior with the world.

"Three quarters of a million acres of Saginaw and Muskegon pine, of riparian rights to the greatest of all inland fisheries, of iron-hatted hills and copper-collared ranges," Ringgold said softly. "How good a salesman are you, Harvey? How much faith in the future do you and your company have?"

"I'd have to sell myself on the idea first. I'd want to see the mining country, make a list of lands."

"The propellor *Napoleon* leaves at dawn. I'll pay your passage and show you around, from Iron Bay to Copper Harbor. Let's have a drink on that."

The bartender served Ringgold's order, but stared blankly at Harvey's request. "Sorry, mister, but I never heard tell of raspberry shrub. What's the base? Rum, brandy——"

"Pure raspberry juice," Harvey said coldly, "with sugar and water."

Ringgold choked on his Monongahela rye. Great howling gales! Promotion of a canal at the headwaters of civilization would require the blind optimism of a raving maniac or a roaring drunk, and look what he had fished up—a teetotal abstainer!

That evening Harvey wrote his employers the first hint of coming events:

> This place is admirably situated for commerce, but the Falls of St. Mary's River are an obstruction to progress. A three-quarter-mile canal here, not costing over $400,000, would enable any lake craft to load at Buffalo and go through to Duluth 600 miles west of here without breaking bulk. Yesterday 3 steamers were lying above and 3 below the rapids in sight of each other waiting for their cargoes to be carted between. The extra expense and the wasted time in conveying freight over the portage is shocking. . . . I leave for the Iron Hills and the Copper Country in the morning. I hope to have startling news for you soon.

11

ADVENTURING BEYOND THE MOON

Ringgold called out the landmarks as the *Napoleon* steamed for the mining camps through the portals of Lake Superior,

Point Iroquois and Gros Cap, and churned across White-fish Bay to coast along the Au Sable Banks, the Grand Marais, where the snows and ice of centuries were piled up in sand dunes that the Indians used to preserve fish and game during the summer. Harvey looked down his New England nose when Ringgold told this story of perpetual iceboxes, but he had to believe in the Pictured Rocks that came next because there they were, miles of painted cliffs that sent a man's imagination into a gallop. Then the *Napoleon* turned Laughing Fish Point and entered Iron Bay for Marquette.

Peter White, another legendary young man, welcomed them onto his new dock. The three of them boarded an ore chariot and drove up into the Marquette Range behind a pair of Kentucky jacks on a suicidal strap-iron railroad. At the Jackson and Cleveland locations, the first holes in the iron hills, they saw hand drills and blasting powder blaze a trail that would lead to world leadership in the Age of Steel by way of the unborn Soo Canal.

But Charles T. Harvey, the traveling salesman of destiny, still peddled Fairbanks Scales to Iron Barons. True, he kept his ears and his eyes open. He shared pasties with Cousin-jacks, cruised timber with Canucks who could spot bird's-eye maple as easily as pine, talked with hematite-browed prospectors, toured hills so magnetic that his compass went crazy and his watch ran out twenty-four hours in as many seconds. On his last day in the Iron Country, he stood at Ispheming, on the height of the land where the Carp River runs down one side to Superior and the Escanaba rushes down the other to Lake Michigan, and he asked Ringgold for map directions.

"Get it fixed on your mind instead of a map," Ringgold said. "You're standing on top of the world, if you can just convince yourself."

12

A TENT NEAR COPPER HARBOR

The *Julia Palmer* ordinarily took fifteen hours bound from Iron Bay to Copper Harbor, but the little steamer ran into heavy weather as the wind hurricaned down from Hudson Bay, and Lake Superior turned into a howling wilderness of waters. Returning to the Main Salon after hours of helping Captain Ryder fight the wheel, Ringgold found a group of passengers singing a hymn of thanksgiving that the propeller had survived the gale. At the other end of the Social Hall, Harvey sat with his feet hooked around a table-leg and a pile of maps under his nose. His outward attitude, from the set of his jaw to the frowning concentration of his high forehead, proclaimed that he could not be bothered with a gale, he had more important matters on his mind, and he preferred to hear his hymns on Sunday, thank you!

Ashore on Keweenaw Peninsula, boomtown miners were sinking shafts through prehistoric pits that had been old diggings long before Columbus had sailed for the new world. From Eagle River to Ontonagon, Harvey exasperated Ringgold by peddling his blasted scales, but he pinned a Cornish sconce to his hat at the Minnesota Mine and went down the hole to see the largest mass of solid copper ever unearthed, more than five hundred tons of pure metal.

"A man-sized nugget," Ringgold said, and he finally forced a showdown as Harvey pored over crude prospecting maps by candlelight in a tent near Copper Harbor.

"All right brother," said Ringgold, "you've seen the elephant and heard the owl. You've listed your choice of lands. What's the answer? Are you going to keep on peddling scales for a living, or start selling the future for America?"

Candle flame etched Harvey's square jaw and hatchet nose. "I have no hankering to be remembered as a huckster of scales," he told Ringgold. "From now on, I'm selling—

the Soo Canal!" He swerved abruptly. "And what about you?"

"I'll tag along," said Ringgold. "I'll be the tail to your kite. If you want any mountains moved, call on me for a cargo of faith. Consider the *Huron Belle* as your private yacht and me as your trouble-shooter. I'm with you until the first ship sails through the canal into Lake Superior."

"The greatest canal in the world!" dreamed Harvey aloud. "And we'll give the *Huron Belle* the honor of being that first historic ship——"

The scene began to strike Ringgold's funny bone. He slapped the patchwork tent and hooted: "Listen to us! A couple of nobodies in the middle of nowhere—fixing to shape the future and make ourselves famous and set the world on its ear!"

Harvey nodded, his face serious. "That makes us the same as most young people," he agreed. "To be different, we've got to succeed!"

BOOK TWO

Erie War

Down a narrow pass they wandered,
Where a brooklet led them onward,
Where the trail of deer and bison
Marked the soft mud on the margin,
Till they found all further passage
Shut against them, barred securely
By the trunks of trees uprooted,
Lying lengthwise, lying crosswise,
And forbidding further passage.

Song of Hiawatha

BOOK TWO

Erie War

1

GAINSBOROUGH PORTRAIT

BACK AT Sault Ste. Marie with Ringgold after their whirlwind inspection tour from Iron Bay to Copper Harbor, Harvey shot a letter to Messrs. Fairbanks that contained far more
than the usual orders of patent scales. He wrote:

> I have now visited every settlement and mine of impor-
> tance in the Lake Superior country. The building of the
> canal mentioned previously is necessary to render available
> the immense latent wealth in minerals there. I feel that
> the undertaking is a vital one to the nation, and should
> also prove profitable to the canal contractors. . . . I ask
> permission to devote myself to promoting the enterprise at
> least so far as to obtain suitable action by the Michigan
> legislature when it meets in January. . . . The time for
> action is at hand.

Harvey took to heart the last line of his letter. With Ringgold's help he immediately began to run a rough survey for
the canal. The news spread fast. Some townspeople came to
jeer, but a more ominous undercurrent was at work. Suddenly, as if by signal, the crews of both portage railroads quit
their jobs and an angry mob led by Cole Slater milled up
Water Street.

Ringgold, squinting over a surveying instrument, spotted
them coming. "Yonder sails trouble, loaded for bear!" he
sang out. "Do we pull up stakes and make tracks for shelter?"

Harvey dropped the measuring chain. "We pull up stakes,"
he rumbled, grabbing a stout oak marker in each fist, "and
we stand our ground!"

"Just wanted the boys to hear the official announcement from their boss," Ringgold flashed his fighting grin at the half-dozen members of the surveying gang. "Let us spare no effort, gentlemen, in seeing to it that our visitors are properly entertained." His jaunty manner tried to hide the grim realities of a situation he understood far better than these newcomers to the North Country who were used to law and order instead of fang and claw.

Slater, a wilderness of a man, had fastened his fortunes to those of his new employer. In Harvey's plan he saw a threat to the Trowbridge Portage Company and to his own lustful schemes. Here he came to manhandle Harvey and his surveyors out of any canal-building notion.

Ahead of Slater's rabble, like a flash of sunlight racing a storm, Susan Marie Beaufait Eldridge Johnston streaked across the meadow to bring warning and reinforcements in the shape of Patrick Flynn, his brawny firemen, and the crew of an Isle Royale schooner bribed with Rumbellion, but it was a buggy driven by Genesee Trowbridge that wheeled between the hostile groups and prevented immediate battle.

Ringgold's eyes sang love lyrics as they watched Genesee bring the matched Canadian ponies to a prancing halt while her father fought for his balance. Daniel Trowbridge seemed stronger than when he had arrived at the Soo, but a shawl protected his shoulders and he wheezed rather than spoke from the buggy seat as he held a watch in his palm and warned:

"You've got five minutes to get the men back on the job, Slater. I appreciate your loyalty, but we can't have violence."

"Why can't we?" Slater growled. "We've got them ten to one, and there's no law to stop us."

A riding whip cracked and a voice cried: "Slater!" Gorgeous as a Gainsborough portrait, her cheeks pinked with excitement, Genesee Trowbridge leaped to her feet. "You heard my father, Slater!"

The blue assurance in her eyes dueled down the green
and shifty deadliness in his. Slater's fists became slack hands.
"You heard what the boss said," he mumbled.

Backed up by the *Huron Belle's* fuel-heavers and Susan
Marie's sailor recruits, Patrick Flynn prodded Slater's dis-
gruntled roustabouts along toward the docks where a battle
royal could be enjoyed by all without any petticoat inter-
ference. "Sure, and you've got your marching orders," he
bellowed, hoisting a whaler's harpoon, "so step lively or I'll
spear ye like fish in a barrel!"

Genesee turned to Harvey and Ringgold. Her voice rang
with scorn. "The pair of you must be crazy—to think you
can build a canal up here at the end of nowhere, a place
hundreds of miles from a railroad, the closest telegraph station
in Detroit, the nearest machine shop in Saginaw, a place
marooned all winter, ice-locked from civilization half the
year, where the temperature dips so far——"

"Then why are you so worried?" Harvey asked, as she
stopped to catch breath.

Sweetly feminine, all her defenses down to him, she told
why: "Because you might succeed in spite of everything. It
would ruin Sault Ste. Marie. The whole town depends on
the portage trade, on entertaining passengers and ship's crews
who stay here while freight is transferred. A canal would
run us all out of business. It would turn this place into a
ghost town."

"You're wrong," Ringgold said, the warmth in him reach-
ing out for her. "You're taking the short view. Listen, Genesee——"

"Miss Trowbridge, sir!" She had played humble with Harvey, but she could blaze out at Ringgold. "You're responsible
for this, you and your boomer bally-hooly——" She checked
her burst of temper, and concluded quietly. "My father and
I will fight any attempt to build a canal at the Soo. We will
fight you to a finish!"

Ringgold cherished the memory of her rounded chin long after the buggy dust had settled. Then his eyes came back from dreaming to notice that Susan Marie Beaufait Eldridge Johnston stood alongside, perking up from her sunbonnet. Remembering, he said, "Thanks for the help, little sister."

Little sister! It drummed at her all the way home. Someday he would be sorry for calling her that! Passing the Van Anden house she made a grotesque face. Also she hoped that someone would get pimples and lose all her hair.

2

CHINESE LANTERN DREAMS

Upstairs in what Landlord Van Anden grandly called the Imperial Suite, Daniel Trowbridge gagged on the cod-liver oil his daughter spooned into him. "Boot polish!" he spluttered. "Typical female trick to shut a man's mouth, but I won't drop the subject. Captain Ringgold has a code of honor, a heart to fight for lost causes, and the soul of a troubadour, but Harvey——he's hungry. Mark my words, he has such an appetite for fame that he doesn't aim to leave room at the table for anyone else, not even a wife. Why favor him?"

"For the reason a woman wants anything, I guess," Genesee said. "Because she hasn't got it."

Her father threw up his hands in surrender. "Oh, I forgot to tell you. I asked Trader Barbeau about renting the old Schoolcraft residence. He anticipated no difficulties and advised me to see the Indian Agent in Detroit when we go below this winter."

Radiant, Genesee hugged him. They would have to spend the winter in Lansing, lobbying against the canal enterprise, but next summer! Already she planned her first lawn party at Elmwood, bright with Chinese lanterns, brilliant with distinguished guests. Young Harvey stood at the top of her invitation list, and even Captain Ringgold would be included.

On returning from the Copper Country, Ringgold had found a mere thank-you note from Cambridge. It irritated him and he sent off a sharp reply:

> ESTEEMED COUSIN: Where is the poem about Lake Superior? Surely, Coz, in receipt of half a ton of books, you could have dashed off a few rhymes in a spare hour or so. When William Cullen Bryant visited Sault Ste. Marie, he sent Whittier only an eagle feather to write ten whole stanzas about St. Mary's Falls, the Pictured Rocks, etc. I am, Coz, disappointedly yours,
>
> Captain Eureka Longfellow Ringgold,
Master, Huron Belle.

It was an impetuous, impertinent letter, but so youthfully human in its hurt outcry that the Harvard professor's eyes twinkled and his beard twitched. He wondered again why any sane father would name his son Eureka, he speculated about the unrecorded Pennsylvania branch of the family, and then he proceeded to spank his alleged kinsman by mail:

> MY DEAR HOTSPUR: This is not a poem factory. Re the Schoolcraft volumes, for which again accept my thanks, you may hear from me in the fullness of time. Meanwhile, I beg to remind you that I am not John Greenleaf Whittier but, as ever,
>
> Henry Wadsworth Longfellow.

3

A VERMONT INVENTOR

While Professor Longfellow penned his brief note to Ringgold from Cambridge, Massachusetts, a prolonged discussion concerning the other member of the canal team began to near its climax in neighboring Vermont.

Although autumn had touched Cambridge, the nip and tang in the air was much sharper in St. Johnsbury. The hills

were paint-splashed with maple leaves. Down Sleeper River
the water ran cold and white-capped to help turn the wheels
of the Fairbanks Scales Factory. In their upstairs office, the
three brothers who had revolutionized the scales industry
were making a final decision on Charles T. Harvey's request
to promote a ship passage between the Lower Lakes and Lake
Superior.

They formed a perfect team, these brothers. Erastus Fairbanks, twice elected Governor of Vermont, was the oldest
brother and the organizing mainspring of the firm. He managed and directed the inventive genius of Thaddeus while the
youngest brother, Joseph, handled the legal end.

While 'Rastus and Joe totaled up figures on canal construction costs, discussed the potential value of Michigan's mineral
and timber lands, and ran a fine-tooth-comb over young Harvey's character and company record (son of a Presbyterian
minister, doesn't drink, smoke or play cards; hard-working,
able, alert, ambitious, been with us about six years now),
Thad stared out the window at the mapled hills. Now, if a
man could figure out a way to use all that color going to
waste. Might sound crazy to some folks, but so did the plow
and the cooling gadget when he was juggling those ideas.
Funny how he lost interest in things once he proved they
would work. Just never renewed the patent on the plow, and
gave the refrigerator away. Guess it was a good thing 'Rastus
took over before he invented the scales. Oh, well, a man
couldn't afford to worry about making money from his inventions. If he did, he wouldn't have time to think up things
to invent. Take this young Harvey. He had watched the
boy and there was a kind of drive and jump to him that never
would be satisfied with staying put. Most men who ever gave
anything to the world were restless. Most countries too.
Losing stuff along the way, sure, but finding better, or in-
venting it.

"Thad!" Erastus Fairbanks called sharply. "Stop day-dreaming!"

"Hmmmmmm? You were saying——Oh, yes. Yes, indeed! Young Harvey's scheme. 'Course I was listening. Never missed a word. Well, now, if you want to know what I think——

"Twenty-five years ago," he said, "there were no platform scales in the world, no telegraph, no sewing machines. We've invented them right here in the United States——just in the time it's taken young Harvey to climb out of diapers. This is a sudden nation. Today, Fairbanks Scales are weighing prairie schooners, Erie Canal barges, ocean leviathans, iron horses; tomorrow, they may be weighing flying ships and even moon machines——"

"Talk sense, Thad!" Joseph Fairbanks rapped the desk irritably.

"Joe's right!" barked Erastus Fairbanks. "Where would this business be today if we wasted time on that brand of foolishness?"

But then, while the walls still echoed their outburst, the eyes of the firm's two practical brothers seemed irresistibly drawn to the fireplace mantel where the miniature model of Thaddeus Fairbanks' first platform scale held the place of honor. The down-to-earth partners exchanged sheepish glances, and turned to the daydreamer.

"Where would this business be today?" asked Erastus. "Nowhere!"

"Agreed," said Joseph. "Keep right on talking nonsense, Thad!"

So, after a period of respectful listening to what most level-headed men of affairs would have called foolishness, the realistic brothers finally steered Thaddeus around to the point at issue—whether to allow their Managing Agent of the Western States to promote a canal.

"I'd give Charles Harvey a chance," Thaddeus said. "But suppose we get an opinion from someone his own age. Happens we've got another young Charles on the payroll. Charles Hosmer Morse. They'll both go a long way. Got the same look in their eyes—as if they could see a whole hundred years ahead. Let's call in Morse and put him on the carpet."

Joseph and Erastus shrugged at each other. There was no use trying to understand Thad's mind, and no sense in opposing him. Besides, however much they might frown at a mere youngster being invited to join them in making an important decision, they had to admit that Morse's background and employment record were excellent. Nephew of Zelotus Hosmer, the first sales agent for Fairbanks Scales, he had studied at neighboring St. Johnsbury Academy until, at seventeen, he had gone into the scale business, binding himself out for three years as apprentice at fifty dollars a year and board. With several weeks of his apprenticeship still to serve, he already had worked up from general helper and clerk to chief accountant in the factory, and was being considered for advancement to the New York office.

Now, answering his summons, he seemed a schoolboy among professors. But he had wide-set eyes, a long firm mouth, and an air of thoughtful calmness that spoke of far-aimed plans and quiet confidence in his power to succeed. This did not keep him from straightening his neckpiece and brushing a hand nervously through his vigorous shock of curly hair as he awaited notice.

"We'll get around to why we sent for you," Thaddeus Fairbanks said. "How do you like the sound of Charles Hosmer Morse?" he asked unexpectedly. "It's a good, strong, bold name. I'll bet you think there's none better. I'll bet you're dreaming about adding it to the firm some day. I'll bet you've practiced writing it down, *Fairbanks, Morse and Company,* until it almost looks real. You started with us from scratch and you've done tolerably well, so I suppose you figure you could run the works yourself by now." He cocked an almighty eyebrow. "Don't answer me, son. When I was twenty I figured I could run the whole world with one hand and guide the universe with the other. You the same as me, getting tired of taking orders?"

Young Morse was bewildered, but not bowled over. "I'm not *tired* of taking orders, Mr. Fairbanks," he replied. "Taking orders is easy work. I'd like a chance at some hard work. I'd like to *give* orders."

Thaddeus nodded approval. "That's the difference, son," he said. "The man in charge has the hard job of making decisions, and his company either profits by them or pays for them, according to how good he is at the business. Happens we've got a decision to make right now, and we've called you in as a kind of junior partner to hear your opinion. You know about our correspondence with Harvey out west. What's your advice, Mis-ter Morse?"

Mr. Morse asked for a few moments of final consideration. Grave as a banker, he paced the carpet. "I think we should use the energies and talents of this young man Harvey to expand our western enterprises," he said in the deepest tones his twenty-year-old nature would allow. "Such a canal is inevitable, and I feel it would be a matter of pride and accomplishment for our company to have had a first hand in its promotion and construction. As the canal opens up commerce, the cities along the Great Lakes shoreline will mushroom to fabulous size." Here his deep tones became lost in shrill notes of boyish excitement. "Take Chicago, for instance. A blind man could look at the map and tell it's bound to become the heart of America and the crossroads of the world. In years to come we may find it wise to shift the center of our operations to such a hub and make it the headquarters of Fairbanks and Company."

"You mean, *Fairbanks, Morse, and Company,* don't you?" Thaddeus Fairbanks said, his chuckle taking any sting out of the jibe.

Young Mr. Morse blushed scarlet, and, given his leave, bolted for the door and disappeared. "Don't smile up your sleeves at the boy," Thaddeus told his brothers. "One of these days he might be boss of the whole works. Charles Morse and Charles Harvey are the kind of young men who will be running, not only this company, but this country of ours some day."

"You and your crazy ideas," Joseph said, shaking his head.

"Let's get down to serious business," Erastus said impatiently.

But then, with one accord, they swiveled around again to the fireplace mantel where a small model of a great invention could be seen. They stared at it long and thoughtfully while Brother Thad went off on another day-dream.

4

BIG EYES

As a result of the unorthodox St. Johnsbury business conference, a letter, signed by Joseph Fairbanks, the lawyer of the firm, reached Sault Ste. Marie on an Indian summer afternoon in October. With Ringgold looking over his shoulder as they stood on the dock alongside the mail boat, Harvey opened the envelope and read:

"Draw on us for the expense of the new venture."

There was more than that to the letter but those were the big, bold words. The Fairbanks Brothers and Charles Hosmer Morse, their make-believe junior partner on Thad's whim, were not contracting to build a canal, not yet; but Harvey had permission to look around and report his findings.

Ringgold let loose an exuberant yell and clapped Harvey on the back. "Now we can really start moving," he bugled. "Lake Superior, we're coming through!"

"Calm down to a roar," said Harvey, his own voice high with excitement. "First we've got to find out what natural resources there are around here for constructing a canal, and second we've got to sell Michigan lawmakers on the idea of passing a Canal Act this winter, and third—"

"Who cares?" interrupted Ringgold. "The important thing is, we've got the go-ahead, and nothing's going to stop us, short of—"

It was Harvey's turn to cut Ringgold short. "Nothing's going to stop us," he said, with no qualifications, and they shook hands on a deal that defied death or disaster of any kind.

Late that November, they were cruising the St. Mary's River in a birchbark canoe, sizing up timber locations and hunting limestone deposits for the masonry of the canal locks.

One morning at Neebish Rapids about twenty miles below the Soo, Harvey stepped from canoe toward shore to inspect a likely rock outcropping. He slipped on the icy footing, upset the canoe, and plunged Ringgold with him down the rapids. They lost their outfits, barely saved their lives, and crawled ashore with the clothes freezing to their backs. They stripped, rubbed themselves tingling dry with cedar, and danced around while wringing out their clothes. Suddenly, at Harvey's embarrassed yip, they dived for the brush.

From the direction of Mackinac Island a Canadian bateau came skimming along the water. An ancient *voyageur* handled the stern paddle, but up in the bow were red hairbows and eyes too everlastingly big to miss anything. Susan Marie Beaufait Eldridge Johnston leaped lightly ashore and tossed two Hudson's Bay blankets into the brush. Around the

fire that the *voyageur* built she started to hang up Harvey's
and Ringgold's clothing.

"Come out and do not be bashful," she called, her laugh
rippling. "Who is it but your Little Sister?"

Red-faced above the trade blankets, they emerged to be
introduced to the gay-sashed ancient who burst into French
Canadian *patois*. "He is Hyacinthe Beauharnais, my godfather, and a great boaster," Susan Marie explained. "He
says: 'I was a good man; no portage was ever too long for me
and no pack ever too large; fifty songs could I sing; I have
saved the lives of ten *voyageurs;* I have had twelve wives and
six running dogs; I spent all my money in pleasure. I am
old and poor now. Were I young again I would spend my
life the same way over.'"

It was Hyacinthe Beauharnais who took them to Drummond Island still farther down the St. Mary's River toward
Lake Huron. He showed them the home he had made for
himself inside what had once been a British fort. There were
his traps, his whitefish nets, his hunting dogs; his swayback
pony and the cutter that whistled him over the ice to the
Soo each winter when his supplies ran low. Here were his
proudest possessions: a cape of glossy pelts made from the
choice prizes of a lifetime in the fur trade, and an ivory miniature of a French girl who might have been Susan Marie.

"My grandmother," she sparkled. "He was madly in love
with her, but she was sister to a *voyageur*. She knew that a
sailor has a sweetheart in every port, but a *voyageur*, ah,
mon brave! he has a honeybee at every portage!"

Hyacinthe Beauharnais nodded and smiled hugely. The
last thing he showed them was his gift to progress: a limestone deposit at the far end of Drummond Island.

Harvey chipped off a specimen. "We'll open our quarry
here," he prophesied boldly. "Imagine finding the stone for

the locks, the siding, most of the masonry for the canal only
half a day from the Soo—"

Susan Marie looked at Harvey. "Do you always count
your chickens before they hatch, m'sieu?"

"There's no thrill in counting them afterwards. The biggest adventure," said Harvey, "is inside the shell, inside a
man's mind—"

"Ah, you are wrong, m'sieu, the biggest adventure is inside the heart."

5

FLATTERING A SOLAR COMPASS

The *Huron Belle,* with Harvey aboard, cleared the Soo for
Detroit early in December. Later, when Lake Superior was
officially closed to navigation, the Trowbridge Portage Company shut down for the winter, and the Trowbridges and
Cole Slater took the last boat out that season from the
shivering huddle of shacks and wigwams on the frozen back
of beyond.

In Detroit, Genesee met stinging disappointment. The
Indian Agent expressed himself as mortified at not being able
to oblige a lady, but a certain Charles T. Harvey already had
taken an option to lease Elmwood.

Daniel Trowbridge squeezed his daughter's hand. "Never
mind," he said. "We'll defeat the Canal Bill and Harvey will
forfeit his option."

During the forty days of the legislative session at Lansing,
Genesee reigned undisputed queen of the state capital. Her
smile alone was a bribe and her eyes could make a politician's
heart jump through hoops.

With Cole Slater as his right-hand man, Daniel Trowbridge, sturdier by the hour, spearheaded the opposition to
the Canal Bill. Powerful political interests ranged themselves against any project as remote on the map and as bare
of voters as the Soo; they had gravy boats to ride closer home.

Also, Michigan had burned her fingers on a Soo Canal contract once before, and many honest politicians were determined to prevent the possibility of suchlike repetition.

"Man alive, that's crazy thinking!" Ringgold roared at one lawmaker. "I suppose if somebody promised you a piece of cake and never delivered it, you'd swear off eating cake forever!"

During those first hectic weeks that winter, Ringgold and Harvey bumped into solid walls of opposition, but they kept bouncing back harder than ever. Sometimes, in their personal calls upon legislators, they shouted down opposing arguments; more often *they* were shouted down.

Only after a staggering procession of sleepless nights spent in studies of surveys and charts and technical data, were they ready to present their canal plans and specifications to Judge William Burt, House Committee Chairman. If Burt could be induced to join their camp, it would mean a big boost toward ultimate success.

On the blustery morning that they scrunched over the snow toward Judge Burt's office in the State House, Harvey rehearsed aloud the way he intended to greet the flint-eyed old Iron Hunter who had fathered all the Lake Superior iron discoveries, from Michigan's Marquette Range to Minnesota Territory's mighty Mesaba.

"Put more butter in your mouth!" coached Ringgold. "If I guess right, you can't spread it on too thick!

"I've still got a strong hunch there's a quirk in the old hardshell's character that may be the key to open a ship canal into Lake Superior," said Ringgold in a stubborn voice that sounded as if he might be trying to silence his own misgivings. "We're gambling that the day he stumbled across those ore outcroppings on Jackson Mountain was the proudest day of his life, not because he'd made the first discovery of iron in the North Country, but because the ordinary compasses in his surveying party went spinning crazy, while his own invention,

the solar compass, kept pointing right and proper at the
poles."

Harvey took a deep breath of crackling cold air.   "Here
we go, partner, win or lose!"

Entering the State House, they stomped the snow from
their boots and shook it from their coats, but they couldn't
shake away the doubts that gave them cold feet as they walked slowly into Judge Burt's office.

The Honorable William Austin Burt glared at them from
behind a desk bulky with business matters.   In his tough
sixties, he showed them a hard-lined face as devoid of senti-
ment as an Ottawa mask hacked from ironwood by toma-
hawk.   He made no effort to rise, and his greeting included
no offer of chairs for visitors.

"I know you both by name, and that's all," he rasped.   "I
can spare you a few minutes, but state the purpose of your
call in brief terms."   He put a huge watch on the desk.   "Remember, gentlemen, time is the one loan that no one can re-
pay!"

Ringgold nodded and swallowed hard.   Nervous as a new
salesman with his first customer, Harvey launched into his
carefully rehearsed speech.

"Judge Burt," he began, "I want to introduce myself—not
as the promoter of a canal—but as the employee of *another*
well-known inventor, Thaddeus Fairbanks, whose great con-
tribution to society has been scales instead of the famous compass that resists magnetic attraction and is therefore indis-
pensable in mining country."

Ringgold, responsible for this whole approach, cringed
at the unblushing flattery.   Judge Burt was no fool.   Those
walrus sounds coming from behind the desk were doubtless
preliminary warnings that would result in the two young up-
starts being kicked bodily from the office.

"Har-rumph!" said Judge Burt, and Ringgold's heart sank
a mile.   "Stop beating around the bush, young man, and get

to the point of this call!" Another walrus sound exploded. "I'm willing to bet you don't really know a smithereen about any of my inventions."

"You not only misunderstand me, sir," said Harvey in ringing tones, "but, what is worse, you fail to appreciate the far-famed importance of your gifts to humanity. Possibly in a few remote corners of the globe," he admitted reluctantly, "in darkest Africa or wildest Borneo, there are unenlightened savages who have not heard about your inventions, but, sir, in the civilized world, who cannot speak eloquently and gratefully about the typographer, the equatorial sextant, and the solar compass?"

"Har-rumph!" snorted Judge Burt. "Fiddle and falderal, young man! You've taken a lesson on how to catch old birds like me—sugar for their tongues, salt for their tails. But I'm not to be caught! Get down to business! Where would a landlubber like yourself have heard about my equatorial sextant?"

"From me!" said Ringgold, stepping forward in quaking boots to play their trump card. "Why Judge, the *Huron Belle* wouldn't set out to cross the Detroit River without one of your equatorial sextants aboard. Speaking of your typographer, we've already decided to install at least one of them in the office to handle business correspondence, as soon as we establish Canal Headquarters at the Soo."

"That so?" Judge Burt worked his shaggy brows, then made more walrus sounds. "Bosh and blarney! Get to the point! And don't make up a story about my solar compass!"

"I don't have to make up a story about it," said Ringgold brashly, "I've got one right here in my buffalo coat." And he pulled a box from his pocket and placed the shining instrument on Judge Burt's desk. "That's what guided Harvey and me from Iron Bay to Copper Harbor, over mining country where an ordinary compass wasn't worth a wooden nickel."

Judge Burt's eyes were suddenly bright on his invention, and all the sternness fled his face to leave a boyish enthusiasm there. "I told them!" he bragged. "They laughed at me because I paid more notice to my little gadget than to discovering a whole mountain of iron. But I told them: *What's the use of finding all the iron in creation if you don't know where you are when you find it? And you wouldn't know where you are, if me and my solar compass weren't around to tell you!*"

As Harvey and Ringgold drew breaths of relief at the transformation, he said, "Sit down, boys, make yourselves comfortable," and opened a desk drawer. "You both sound like sensible young fellows," he told them. "I don't show this to just anybody at all, but I think you'll appreciate a trifling award of merit I picked up at the World's Fair."

With due respect Ringgold and Harvey handled the imposing certificate that read:

Hyde Park, London, October 15, 1851
I hereby certify that her majesty's commissioners, upon the award of the jurors, have presented a prize medal to Wm. A. Burt, for a Solar Compass and surveying instrument shown in the exhibition.
ALBERT, President of the Royal Commission.

"Handed it to me himself," Judge Burt said. "Prince Albert, Queen Victoria's husband, you know. Right there in the Crystal Palace. He was wearing one of those coats—"

When the conversation finally wore around to the canal, they presented him with their survey, their report on strategic materials—including timber and the Drummond Island limestone deposits—their plans and specifications for the canal locks.

Judge Burt looked, then he listened. "I'll back you to the hilt," he promised at last. "I'm Chairman of the Committee and they'll see things my way or else! You're a pair of pushing rascals, but it takes brass and bumption to promote a

ditch in the wilderness, and—I'm partial to flattery." His
eyes twinkled. "You both remind me of young Doug Hough-
ton who first put the Copper Country on the map. He had
so much confidence in himself that he challenged a Lake
Superior storm in a rowboat. May he rest in peace, and may
you prosper!"

Outside the State House a few minutes later, two boister-
ous spirits celebrated with a fast-and-furious snow fight that
shocked the lawmakers and tempted lighter-hearted legislators
to join the fun.

Ringgold packed a snowball fit to feed cannons. "Watch
out for that stovepipe lid of yours, brother!" he warned. "I'm
firing a broadside!"

Plunk! His own hat went sailing into the street, and Harvey yelled in triumph just as a sleigh bearing the Trowbridges
jingled up to the State House, Genesee rosy-cheeked in the
crisp air and pretty as a Valentine.

"A fine sight!" growled Daniel Trowbridge. "There's the
type of men who want to build a canal!"

"Yes, I know, Father," agreed Genesee, but her eyes were
sweet and warm as honey in the sun as they followed Harvey's
every move.

Later, looking like walking snowmen, the two partners
skylarked up the street to call on more legislators.

"But we'll never get another prize like Judge Burt," said
Ringgold.

"I didn't have much hope of snaring him," confessed Harvey. "Not with your crazy scheme."

"You've heard about the kingdom that was lost all because
of the loss of a horseshoe nail," grinned Ringgold. "Well,
brother—" he patted the box in his buffalo-coat pocket—
"maybe we'll build the Soo Canal on the strength of this solar compass I borrowed last night!"

6

WILDCAT BY THE TAIL

Their soaring balloon of optimism took a nose dive only a few days later. When the *Detroit Free Press* of January 29, 1853, reached Lansing, the roof blew off the town and came down, kerplunk! on canal hopes. The newspaper carried the complete text of a long open letter from Eber Brock Ward to Judge Burt, and it blasted Harvey's recommendations for a canal to smithereens. In less than an hour Trowbridge and Slater and the whole anti-canal crowd had plastered every hotel lobby and bar in Lansing with the one paragraph in Ward's letter that best suited their purpose:

> The crooked, narrow, shallow and rocky channels in the St. Mary's River will forever deter the largest class of steamers from navigating these waters.

Harvey paced the parlor of his boarding house, slapping the paper, and growing madder every minute. "Who does this pipsqueak Ward think he is?"

Ringgold had just come in, but he had a quick answer for that one. "Ward? Oh, he's nobody much. He just owns more shipping than anybody else on the Great Lakes!"

"Ulp!" All the wind went out of Harvey. "I guess *we're* the pipsqueaks," he muttered dismally. "What do we do now?"

"Talk back to the older generation," Ringgold said, more cheerfully than he felt. "This is the everlasting disagreement between the conservatism of age and the recklessness of youth. Now, don't worry. It's your name that's splashed all over the paper, but I'm responsible for what old Cap Ward's hollering about. I got us into this mess; let's hope I can get us out!" He jammed on his hat. "We better hustle over to the State House, and figure things out on the way."

The situation boiled down to this: Multimillionaire Ward was not against a canal—he was against what he called Har-

vey's extravagant ideas of one. In offering the land grant to
Michigan, the Federal Government had specified a canal with
locks two hundred and fifty feet long and sixty feet wide.
Why, in the name of common sense, was this young whip-
persnapper of a traveling salesman recommending locks three
hundred and fifty feet long by seventy feet wide? Did he
want to ruin all chances of a canal with his inflated ideas?

As soon as they entered the State House, Judge Burt called
Harvey and Ringgold upon the capitol carpet. He had a face
as long as an unpaid bill. "Boys," he said, "you'd better have
the right answers!" and he hurried them along the corridor
to where a joint meeting of the special committees of both
Houses had been ordered hastily as soon as Captain Ward's
letter was made public. Once the door opened to show what
Judge Burt had brought in, red-faced politicians jumped to
their feet and hurled angry questions:

"Why didn't you have sense enough to submit your plans
to Captain Ward?"

"Where did you get your engineering figures?"

"How much experience have you had, Harvey?"

"Yeah! How many canals have you built?"

A scornful hoot: "You mean, how many birdbaths, don't
you?"

Harvey faced his first crisis squarely, the way he always
faced trouble, with no excuses, and all the weight on his own
shoulders.

"I'm sorry if any harm has been done by the unfortunate
publicity, gentlemen. I assume full blame."

"You'll assume no such thing!" Ringgold strode to the conference table and dueled the whole roomful of politicians
with his eyes. "I'm the one who upped those figures, and
I'm here to tell you Captain Ward's all wrong!"

Again the scornful hoot: "Oho? And how many ships do
you have in your line, Commodore?"

"One," said Ringgold quietly. "But don't forget that old Cap Ward started out as a cabin boy. I respect him. He once had the cold nerve to run a ship down the Soo Rapids from Lake Superior into Lake Huron—and only a handful of men have lived to tell that story. But his days for taking risks are past. As far as the Lakes go, he's a has-been, he's behind the times. Like most old men, he's stopped growing up with the country, and he's begun to spread out—with his stern sheets glued to a Detroit office chair and his eye to the safest profits."

Ringgold cracked the conference table with a fist like a mahogany block. "But this is a young country, gentlemen, and we can't afford to limp behind the times with graybeards. We've got to ride up at the head of the parade. We aren't planning a ditch where schoolboys can huff and puff their toy sailboats—we're planning a man-size canal!"

His voice surged with youthful exuberance. "Not for Fulton's first Hudson River teakettle or that Great Lakes boiler on a raft, the old *Walk-in-the-Water,* but for today's big steamers and for tomorrow's still bigger ones! My answer to Captain Ward is this: "It's easier to dredge a narrow channel than to try to stretch canal locks. I'd rather start with an idea a little too big than wind up with a canal a little too small!"

Judge Burt chuckled and swept the meeting with his iron-gray brows. "All right, boys, that's good enough for me. I'm no old fogy. Let's start drafting that canal bill so we can put it up to the Legislature for a vote."

Afterward, the grizzled Iron Hunter buttonholed Ringgold and Harvey in the cloakroom. "I hope," he said with a genial wink, "that you returned it in good shape."

"Huh?" said Harvey.

"Returned what?" asked Ringgold.

"That solar compass you borrowed from Cap Sparhawk!" said Judge Burt, and left them flopping their mouths like fish out of water.

Even after the Captain Ward strategy fizzled, the anti-canal crowd kept hammering away, with Daniel Trowbridge their acknowledged leader. On the final day, after more than a month of lobbying, he took the State House floor to address Michigan's assembled Legislature, and there presented the main arguments of the opposition: There was no need of a Soo Canal; the portage companies could handle the business; this was another land grab and stock swindle in the making and, furthermore, it would be impossible to build a canal at what experts called the fag end of creation.

"It's been tried before," Trowbridge reminded the lawmakers. "More than ten years ago canal contractors went to the Soo. When they found out what kind of job they were up against, they skipped with the money advanced to them. That lesson cost this state thousands of dollars—"

When Harvey took the floor in rebuttal, a young woman in the gallery listened with divided heart. Then, in full appreciation of Captain Ringgold's rare sense of destiny, Harvey yielded the floor to him for the clinching argument.

"In spite of all opposition," declared Ringgold, "this legislature is going to launch an endless bridge of ships through the Soo Canal into Lake Superior and thereby open up the true Northwest Passage. This legislature will vote to build a canal across Michigan's Mighty Mile, the most important mile on earth, the gateway toward a greater America and a better world—"

Next day the Michigan Canal Act was indeed voted into law, but the Trowbridge faction had inserted a clause that was a guillotine poised over the heads of any contractors. Instead of accepting the Federal Government's allowance of seven years to complete the canal, Michigan had chopped the time limit to two years. Failure to meet the deadline meant no payment in lands; in fact, it meant financial disaster to the backers.

"Two measly years!" said Ringgold as he and Harvey boarded the stage from Lansing. "We've got a wildcat by the tail and no room to swing it!"

"I'll soft-pedal that in my report," said Harvey, and he boomed into Detroit for a telegraphic showdown with the Fairbanks Brothers. It was the rough end of a bleak winter by then, and he had been going full-tilt since autumn, but he still had the bumption and bounce to make the wires hot with optimistic answers to their long-distance doubts:

Could the canal be finished within the time limit? Take his word for it! Were the mineral and timber lands sufficiently valuable to warrant this gamble? They could bank on his lists! Could he send them the names of Michigan capitalists ready to act as securities? He grandly endorsed the kind of presidents he had sales-talked while the nation elected Pierce—presidents whose names were institutions: Michigan Central Railroad, Detroit Savings Bank, Merchants' Navigation Company, Detroit Dry Dock Company, Michigan Insurance Bank, Wyandotte Iron and Steel Company. He had names to knock their eyes out!

"Do these men know you're using their names?" Ringgold asked, whistling at sight of one telegram. "Never mind, don't answer me!"

Harvey, overcoming all objections, kept the wires humming as March winds howled and shrilled from Detroit to St. Johnsbury. Finally, sold on the enterprise by their own salesman, the Fairbanks Brothers invited New York and New England entrepreneurs to join them in taking the contract and, with young Harvey on the spot to represent the Easterners, Michigan accepted them as the contractors on April 5, 1853. It marked a red-letter day on the Great Lakes. Patrick Flynn and Captain Ringgold asked Harvey to join their celebration, at the Black Horse Inn, and he was as high on success and raspberry shrub as they were on Rumbellion.

7

DIRTY WORK AFOOT

That same evening, after banishing Genesee to the lobby, Daniel Trowbridge summoned Cole Slater to the Van Buren suite in the National Hotel. He served his guest a bouquet glass of peach-flavored *L'Eustrope,* Detroit's famous old *habitant* favorite. As Slater gulped, Trowbridge sipped, staring out the window at Cadillac Square, and at the flickering gas lamps on Woodward Avenue. His voice was slow, deliberate.

"A Soo Canal would bankrupt me, Slater. I'm too old to start from scratch. I've got my daughter to protect. Do you think Harvey has a chance?"

"With weather and wilderness against him, and men like me who know how to help Nature along?" Slater grinned wickedly. "I'm betting he won't make his deadline."

"I was thinking we might discourage his backers and persuade them to drop the project before they sink any real money into it. Either that, or force them to make a deal with us!" Trowbridge pointed out what everyone knew: that news of a canal had sent values soaring; that hordes of speculators were swarming the water-front hotels, waiting for navigation to open so they could rush up into Lake Superior and buy lands in wholesale lots.

"Yeah, but they're Johnny-come-latelies compared with Harvey," Slater growled. "He's got lists of the choicest stuff in the Upper Peninsula. Soon as the ice breaks, he'll board the first boat to the Soo and withdraw the lands from sale. He's got the jump!"

"Unless we steal a march on him. Unless we secure his lists somehow, and enter them ourselves at the Soo Land Office, and notify Fairbanks Brothers that we already own the valuable mineral properties they were counting on." Trow-

bridge stared at Slater. "I can get plenty of financial backing, and we've got a silent partner up there in the Land Office
who'll cut a few corners for us, but the real job's up to you.
I've chartered the steamer *Northerner*. Captain Sweet thinks
he can get us as far as Mackinac—"

Slater's eyes glistened as if they were already counting the
gold pieces. "Double my wages," he said, "and forget your
worries about those lists!"

8

STEAMBOAT RACE

As dawn began to snuff out the stars, three young merry-
makers came frolicking home from the Black Horse Inn.
They harmonized "Yea, yea, yea, in Michigan-i-a!" up the
stairs of the Exchange Hotel and into Harvey's suite but there
the song died in their throats. The rooms had been turned
upside down. Even the beds were wrecked. The ornate tops
of the brass bedposts blinked at them from the floor. Harvey
scrooged his fingers into the hiding place in one of the posts.
His hand came out empty, and so were his eyes.

"The land lists!" he cried. "Gone!"

"Maybe not too far gone," Ringgold whirled on Flynn.
"Get steam up in your boilers, mister, and rip off the safety
valve! It's time to travel!"

At peep of day the *Huron Belle* steamed up the Detroit
River and into Lake St. Clair with the drift ice snapping at
her bow and Captain Ringgold wheeling her through. Harvey gloomed out at the frozen shoreline, a copy of the original
land lists in his pocket but not much hope in his heart. They
were five hours behind the fast steamer *Northerner*. Ringgold jingled the engine room for more speed. Down below,
Patrick Flynn, who was mixing pitch and turpentine with
his cordwood, heaved a barrel of lard into the fire. As flames
whooshed out, the Irishman beamed and tested the boilers
with a spray of Crabapple Cut Plug.

"Bulging, but not busting," was his verdict to a panic-eyed fireman. "Better hoist another drumhead of cheese to hold down that safety valve. She's on the prod to blow off steam!"

At Port Huron, waterside watchers shouted that the *Northerner* had a good four-hour lead. The sidewheeler bowled along the Thumb toward the top of Michigan's mitten. She lurched across stormy Saginaw Bay that caught every capful of wind and cupful of sea on the Great Lakes, and that night the sparks from her stacks threw new stars in the sky, but she was still more than three hours behind.

Abreast of the Straits of Mackinac the next day, Harvey sighted steamer smoke dead ahead, but Ringgold doused his hopes by saying it must be the *Northerner* on the return trip. And so it was, with Genesee Trowbridge picture-framed on the deck between Captain Sweet and her father. Radiant as a Snow Carnival Queen, she waved one hand gaily from her muff as the steamers almost brushed in passing.

Ringgold kissed his fingers to her in French salute. "Cheer up," he told the glowering Harvey. "The race isn't over yet. What they've done, they put Slater ashore up ahead on the Snowshoe Pike from Mackinac to the Soo. He's a fast man on webs and the overland route is shorter by a third, but I'm chancing the river."

He threaded the *Huron Belle* into the frosty mouth and down the frozen throat of the St. Mary's until her bow thumped into a solid wall of ice and her paddle wheels churned in vain. Then he called Patrick Flynn up to the wheelhouse and said: "Take over, mister!" He gripped Harvey's hand and pocketed the copy of the land lists. Over the bow of the *Huron Belle* he went, and up the river road in a shuffling snowshoe run.

He was at least two hours behind Cole Slater, and he had chosen the long way around, but he figured that Drummond Island lay only a league ahead. Within half that distance his ankles were sore and swollen from the pace he had set, but worse torture was the suspense. Suppose Hyacinthe Beauharnais had driven his cutter into Sault Ste. Marie for fresh supplies. Suppose—

"*Bejou!*" called an ancient *voyageur* in nor'wester greeting from a Drummond Island headland, and in no time the god-father of Susan Marie had his swaybacked pony hitched to the old cutter. *Hoh, hoh! En avant!* Off they flew on the river road with the cutter crisping over the snow and the pony's shoes ringing on ice. Would they reach the Soo before Cole Slater? *Hoh, hoh! Roulant ma boule!* In a whistle of wind and a jingle of bells, they whisked off the river road on-to Water Street and Ringgold ran for the Land Office. He slapped Harvey's lists on the counter. "Withdraw those lands from sale!"

Slater stumbled into the Soo off the Snowshoe Pike fifteen minutes too late. When he saw Ringgold, his black-whisk-ered face fell apart. "You!" he croaked in disbelief.

"Me, and smiling out loud," said Ringgold. "You can eat those lists you stole, Slater. The canal contractors have re-served the lands."

What lands? Ringgold and Slater had raced for what la-ter turned out to be two of the richest prizes in history. Lo-cated on Harvey's lists, among other treasure-troves, were Cleveland Cliffs, greatest iron ore producer of the Marquette Range, and Calumet & Hecla, most fabulous of all native copper mines. By guess or by golly, the salesman of scales had put his map finger where the two Michigan giants would rise to pay hundreds of millions of dollars in dividends.

9

RED SKIES

While Ringgold treated Hyachinthe Beauharnais to the best keg of Napoleon at the Soo, he watched a blizzard blot out the landscape and braced himself for weeks of suspense that would last until the *Huron Belle* brought Harvey back from his trip East to secure an Albany charter and help organize the canal company on Wall Street.

Harvey had his own worries about Ringgold, but he had to go ahead in the dark and count on his partner's success against Slater. There were a million things to do, and they should have been done yesterday, so he had no time to spare for thoughts of failure.

Not trusting the ice jams in shallow Lake Erie, he left the *Huron Belle* in Patrick Flynn's safekeeping at Detroit and took the Michigan Southern to Toledo. There he had to shift baggage, buy a different ticket, and board another train for Cleveland. It was the same story all the way along the line. Travelers grumbled, but they shifted baggage, bought new tickets, and boarded a different string of cars at every whistle stop. He thought no more of the inconvenience than any other passenger, until he rode straight into the Erie War that spotlighted a problem of his own at Sault Ste. Marie.

When Harvey's train arrived, the night skies were red over Erie, Pennsylvania. An aroused citizenry had torn up new railroad tracks for bonfires. The Governor of Pennsylvania had declared a state of martial law, but the militia hobnobbed with the rioters who were led by Erie's mayor and the county sheriff. Harvey pushed his way through the mob to his next train. What was all the trouble about? Would someone please tell him?

Sure thing, stranger. You know what that railroad company's trying to do? Make the tracks that lead out of here the same size as the ones that lead into here. They can't do that to Erie, Pennsylvania! You take now, trains have to stop on account of one runs on a different size track, so folks have to change cars and wait around awhile, maybe overnight even. That means plenty of business for hotels, eating places — prosperity for Erie. But you take now, if they made the tracks the same size, the trains wouldn't have to stop for anything, folks would go straight on through without spending a dime, just stare out the coach windows at us, and this would be a ghost town. You can bet your boots we aren't going to let that happen, stranger. We've declared war—Erie War!

As he reached the next station and boarded another train of cars, Harvey looked back at the flaming Erie skyline. He had felt the temper of the mob, decent people as individuals, but itching to beat progress over the head and burn it at the stake because they were afraid it might hurt their pocketbooks and bypass their city. All along, the Connecticut Yankee had considered any antagonism toward the canal as fantastic. The Erie War gave him a clearer understanding of the hostile attitudes. It also showed him how far the Trowbridges and their supporters might go in opposing a Soo Canal.

At Albany he secured a charter from the state legislature, telegraphed his employers, and—before April bowed to May —arrangements were made with all interested parties for a meeting at the corner of William and Wall Streets in New York City to organize the St. Mary's Ship Canal Company.

10

TALLEST BUILDINGS ON MANHATTAN

An earnest young man, wearing the shawl and beaver hat that proclaimed him a New York office worker, met Harvey at the station. "Charles Hosmer Morse at your service," he announced. "I'm your welcoming committee from the Fairbanks Brothers, and delegated to see that you get a good lunch before we invade the wilds of Wall Street."

He led the way to an oyster bar, but Harvey traced canal figures on the table with his fork and showed no interest in food. Young Mr. Morse, by natural instinct, took him in charge.

"Eat," he said. "Every scrap on your plate. You need the strength, and besides, there's no sense in waste. Are you nervous about the meeting?"

"Nervous?" Harvey echoed. "Of course not," he denied instantly, but then he met the candid glance of the other. "Nervous?" he said. "I'm scared."

"I felt the same way when I was transferred here not long ago," young Mr. Morse admitted. "My family bought me this shawl and beaver hat so I'd look the same as a typical New York businessman. But it didn't stop the Fairbanks clerks from making fun of me as a country boy. They laughed at what I wore and what I said and what I did. They almost laughed me out of the city. I sat down on a curbstone one day, homesick as a boy could be, and fought the question out with myself. Should I stay here or go back to St. Johnsbury? I sat on that curbstone until I felt taller than any building on Manhattan. I made up my mind that someday I'd show the people in the New York office how a business should be run. And I wouldn't stop at scales either."

Harvey could only stare, gulp his oysters as commanded, and ask: "What do you mean, you wouldn't stop at scales?"

"When my name is added to the company," said young Mr. Morse with sublime confidence, "I'll expand our operations into an all-around industrial concern. I'm interested in power, steam power, wind power, whatever kind of power may be invented or discovered. This is the machine age, and when I get my say, our company will start producing the motors and engines for it." He gave a sudden glance across the table. "Wild dreams?"

"I'm not in very good shoes to call anyone's dreams wild," said Harvey. "You've given me the boost I needed," he continued, and added with one of his rare smiles, "I feel like the second tallest building on Manhattan."

But when the two young men with the same first name entered the meeting place at William and Wall, the optimism inspired by Charles Hosmer Morse's faith in his own destiny was soon drained from Charles T. Harvey. He made himself small at a teakwood table, sitting in awed silence except when called upon for information, humbled in an atmosphere of ruby port and long-ashed Havanas.

These capitalists that the Fairbanks Brothers had invited to join the enterprise were more than men to him; they were portraits in oils to hang on counting-house walls; they were tea clippers beating up the windward passage in the China trade; they were whalers out of New Bedford for Thar-she-blows; they were names to roll on the tongue and savor like a rare wine—August Belmont of New York, John M. Forbes of Boston, Thomas Dwyer of Dwyer's Landing; they were names with the ring of fame and money—John F. Seymour, Benjamin Tibbits, John V. L. Pruyn, Henry Dwight, Jr.; they were names to call a *Who's Who in Michigan and the West* —James F. Joy of Detroit, Henry P. Baldwin of Grosse Point, John Owen of Old Fort Shelby, George F. Porter of Grosse Ile, Franklin Moore of Wayne County; they were names to put on cigar bands, street markers, park gates, even on city limits; and here at the same table sat a mere traveling sales-man with his name still to make, an unknown with nothing in his pockets but his hands.

Charles Harvey held himself rigid as the meeting pro-gressed, but in spirit he slid lower and lower in his chair. Even with one eye closed he could see two governors and an ambassador. He heard the President of the New York Cen-tral Railroad, Erastus Corning, the President of the Michigan Central, John W. Brooks, and the President of Fairbanks Scales, Erastus Fairbanks, elected to head the officers and directors of the new canal company. One important office remained unfilled, but he felt far from hopeful when his employers suggested their salesman as General Agent.

The big men rubbed chins, pulled noses, stared at Harvey in cold-eyed doubt. The young fellow had done a creditable job of promotion, but this was the key post in the whole works. Involved almost unlimited executive powers and control of large sums in cash and credit. What security could he offer?

Harvey squared his shoulders and set his jaw against disappointment. What could he offer? The plans in his head, the hopes in his heart, the dreams in his soul? Not negotiable!

Then Thaddeus Fairbanks whispered with his two brothers and with young Charles Hosmer Morse before he rose and said quietly: "My associates and I are new to Wall Street and its ways. However, although we come from a small place in Vermont, we make scales for the world. We think we know how to weigh the worth of a man. Our firm is willing to be Mr. Harvey's surety for one hundred thousand dollars——"

11

KISSING TROUBLE

With Harvey gone, a long line of days had stumbled through worry and bad weather for Ringgold. He had pictured a hundred things gone wrong—from international crisis to business slump—all capable of canceling the canal project. As the last snowstorm melted and the warm Chinook winds jammed the St. Mary's River with Lake Superior icebergs church-steeple high, he still fretted because the usual floods downstate were blocking all overland communications, and he imagined that cold-blooded financiers were squeezing Harvey out of the canal deal.

The first week of navigation that season found him dock-prowling and anxious-eyed, but he never heard the *Huron Belle* blow for a landing, and Harvey's coming caught him by surprise. One afternoon late in May, on a short fishing trip to take his mind off worry, he fought his way deep into the brush until he reached a trout hole on a feeder creek.

On his first cast a huge sun-speckled fish lunged half out of water at the Coleman Wriggler, and bear-trap jaws snapped shut on the artificial fly. Ringgold's rod bent double and his fingers burned as the line sang out. Oblivious to all else, he pitted his skill against sixteen pounds of breakneck fury until:

"Careful!" warned someone behind him. "Don't give him an inch of slack or he'll head around that log and——"

Ringgold turned quickly. "Harvey!" he yelled, almost dropping his rod, and enough slack ran out to let the fish dart around the log and snap the line. Ringgold stared in dismay at a flirted tail and a flash of swimming sunshine. "There goes," he said, slowly, "the biggest brook trout ever hooked this side of an opium-eater's dream. Your news better be good!"

Harvey leaped to the edge of the beaver dam beside Ringgold. "Partner," he said, his smile a mile wide, "shake hands with Mr. Charles T. Harvey, General Agent, St. Mary's Falls Ship Canal Company, Sault Ste. Marie, Upper Peninsula, Michigan!"

Ringgold's yell of triumph awoke echoes in the Porcupine Mountains, and when he finally came back to earth, his grip would have crushed lesser bones. "Reporting for duty, boss. What's first on the list?"

"Canal workers," said Harvey. "As many as you can carry, as fast as you can get them up here, and I don't care how or where you get them."

Ringgold nodded. "Count on it, mister. Let's get back to the Soo and start moving."

The two men, big-chested, broad-shouldered, iron-jawed, horizon-eyed, broke through the brush like bull elks. Harvey began to laugh, half to himself, half to Ringgold. "They told me to get things humming," he chuckled. "You see, they

intend to appoint a chief engineer and a superintendent of
construction as soon as they can find the right-caliber men."

Ringgold started laughing too and then, for a side-splitting
moment that showed how young they were, the two of them
whooped and hollered and slapped each other on the back,
for the two right-caliber men were already on the job, and
if any Eastern contractors thought different, the joke was on
them.

"We'll show them," said Harvey.   "Wait'll they get my
first report."

He sent it off that same week:

> Canal Headquarters, June 4, 1853
>
> GENTLEMEN: Arrived here with 400 men plus tools,
> supplies, etc. on steamers *Illinois* & *Huron Belle* 4 days
> ago.   Had shanties erected, men housed within 48 hours.
> Commissary now organized to provide regular meals. Have
> begun hospital on Rapids Island, opened quarry on Drum-
> mond Island, located logging camp at Garden River, etc.
> Have occupied Elmwood, former residence of historian
> Schoolcraft, thus providing excellent quarters and cuisine
> for shareholders & directors who wish to visit here & in-
> spect works.   Pleased to report I will break ground on
> canal today & wheel first barrow from cut to dump. . . .

There was little ceremony at the Soo when Harvey grasped
the brand-new Number Two shovel handed him by Ringgold. "We'll start digging our ditch here and now," he said,
as he stepped on the shovel and turned the first spade of
earth.

Only the Shanty Irish, led by Patrick Flynn, hoisted a
cheer—and divil a bit did they care what happened as long
as they got their fifty a month and food. The anti-canal crowd
waited for a cue from the Trowbridges. Cole Slater bared
his stained teeth and violence baked in his eyes.

Not for twelve more days could Harvey celebrate his twenty-fourth birthday. He had never built so much as a wooden sidewalk. But, against the gloomy backdrop of the Laurentian Range, he loaded the first wheelbarrow with Cambrian sandstone to haul it from cut to dump.

Genesee Trowbridge refused to make room for him. Hands on hips, she blocked his path. Even the ostrich plumes in her Leghorn hat seemed defiant. He could have gone around her, but Harvey never steered around anything if he could enjoy a head-on collision.

"I know you," he said. "You're Erie, Pennsylvania, in person, and pleasanter on the eyes, but you can't block progress."

Quicker than thought he dropped the wheelbarrow to span her waist with his hands, lift her aside, and kiss her startled red lips in the process. The kiss signified nothing but a young man's impulse to put a young woman in her place, and that's what made her furious, but her fingers flew to Slater's sleeve as he made a threatening motion toward Harvey.

"I'll handle him," Genesee whispered, and, oh, how she wished she could.

At the edge of the crowd, a jumping-jack of a girl narrowly watched a young lake captain who claimed Longfellow for his cousin. "I saw your eyes turn from blue to green," said Susan Marie Beaufait Eldridge Johnston. "I saw them both turn green as turtles when he kissed her!"

Captain Eureka Longfellow Ringgold glared hopelessly at her. Miss Mischief was at the difficult age, a little too old for a spanking and a little too young for the treatment given Genesee—or so he thought.

A tense moment followed the kiss. Then Harvey shouted working orders to his crew, and their shovels flashed in the sun behind him. He gripped the wheelbarrow again, and, looking neither right nor left, sang out:

"Gangway, we're coming through!"

He might have been warning the surly pack of portage employees that drew back snarling to give him passage, while a young woman with a green parasol and a girl with red hair bows watched history in the making. Or, in Ringgold's style, he might have been talking to the Falls of St. Mary's roaring down from Lake Superior.

"We got business with white pine and red iron ore, coin copper and Glasgow bonnet wheat . . . . Stand aside for the future!"

BOOK THREE

Michigan Horseshoe

Issued from his lodge of snow-drifts,
From his home among the icebergs,
And his hair, with snow besprinkled,
Streamed behind him like a river,
Like a black and wintry river,
As he turned and hurried southward
Over frozen lakes and pinelands.

Song of Hiawatha

BOOK THREE

Michigan Horseshoe

1

DEAD MEN'S BONES

ALL THE WAY up the rippling St. Mary's, Captain Ringgold heard the Indian drums pulse from both the American and Canadian sides of the river. He scowled at puffs of signal smoke and flashes of medicine mirrors on the headlands, and he rang Patrick Flynn to put more steam behind the paddle wheels. A fine reception for newcomers, he thought sourly, and wondered what mischief had brewed while he had been down the lakes to pick up men and machinery for the canal works. The decks of the *Huron Belle* were jammed with recruits who already were kicking themselves for giving up safe jobs to take foolish chances on the raw rim of danger at the jumping-off place of the world—Sault Ste. Marie, Michigan.

As Ringgold berthed the *Huron Belle* below the rapids and shouldered his way through the mob on McKnight's dock, he picked up the whole story in a glance and listen. The Commandant of Fort Brady had its puny garrison on parade in a brave show of bayonets. Alarm wildfired up Water Street that the Ojibways were on the warpath to avenge the desecration of their forefathers' graves.

"They'll wipe us out!" Cole Slater prophesied to a gang of canallers who had scrambled out of the cut to buy bottled courage. "See those savages gathered on the Canuck shore? They'll leave this town naked as the palm of a man's hand! And who's responsible? Harvey and his canal! The devil and the ditch he's blasting straight through their sacred cemetery."

The black-whiskered general manager of Trowbridge Portage figured he had the perfect setup. He could frighten half these greenhorns into taking the next boat down the lakes; the other half would follow him and rip Harvey's canal company into a hole in the scenery. Slater had no worries about an Indian uprising.

Most of the drums were talking because he had fired up the young chiefs with whisky. They would put on a show, that was all.

Ringgold fathomed Slater's scheme, but his thoughts went deeper, and he feared one spark might touch off an explosion that could blow the Soo off the map. There were dead men's bones involved in this. Primitive loyalties.

Before the *Soo Sentinel* building, Publisher Jay Bisby held thin-lipped conversation with Daniel Trowbridge and other businessmen. The pressure of unfriendly eyes reminded Ringgold that none of Harvey's lieutenants could escape the resentment caused by their efforts to get around the Falls of St. Mary's into Lake Superior with a canal, thus abolishing the slow and costly portage traffic, unfortunately the Soo's main course of income.

"Captain Ringgold, sir!" Sweet-lined and trim as a Baltimore Clipper, Genesee Trowbridge in Empress Eugenie silk sailed through a buckskin-and-homespun mob. Her blue eyes were troubled, milky teeth nipped a red-ripe lip. "I beg you and Mr. Harvey to believe that my father never gave whisky to those Indians——"

Ringgold said he believed, but his heart tripped up his tongue, and he could think of nothing to say to hold the girl in conversation. Then Harvey pushed through the throng, and Genesee's eyes turned immediately to his.

The Connecticut Yankee had a brisk nod for her, a bone-crushing grip for Ringgold. The two young men measured each other with fighting smiles. "Looks like the lid's about to blow off," Harvey told him.

"My watch is always set for a fight. Got any plans?"

Before Harvey could reply, a shout went up as a war canoe shot into midstream from the Canadian shore. An old chief wearing feathered headgear and bear-claw ornaments posed stiffly between paddlers painted for the scalp dance. A thousand pairs of anxious eyes watched that birchbark, graceful as a waterfowl, skim the waves toward Fort Brady. Only a few turned to see Susan Marie Beaufait Eldridge Johnston, sedate for once in her life, lead an elderly Indian woman down toward the stockade gate.

"You are both invited to attend," the girl stopped to tell Ringgold and Harvey. "My great-grandmother has consented to speak to Chief Shegud and his young firebrands."

"Oh?" Genesee gazed in thinly veiled amusement at the swarthy squaw in trade calico and beaded leggings. "And I suppose your great-grandmother—whoever she is—will put an end to this uprising?"

"But of course!" flashed Susan Marie over a pert shoulder. "Why else would such a lady appear in public and expose herself to the gabble of geese?"

Genesee's color heightened. "You'd think," she remarked, "that the saucy little savage held Queen Victoria by the hand."

"Lake Superior's Victoria," Ringgold said proudly. "Schoolcraft called Mrs. John Johnston the Pocahontas of the Northwest, the Ojibway princess who married an Irish nobleman——"

Sault Ste. Marie's almost forgotten relic of wilderness royalty passed through the stockade and waited at the gate for Chief Shegud and his warriors. Along Water Front Street the psychic Irish were first to crowd inside Fort Brady. They cared nothing for the soldiers drawn up at attention, the Commandant with hand to sword hilt, the grave-frocked missionaries. Their eyes were pinned on the venerable princess and the chief of a vanishing race, and on the girl who interpreted the strange murmur of a dying tongue:

Whist, Paddy, and would you look at them now, the ham-
mered copper and the wrinkled leather of them, older than
the brows of Donegal the both of them, but with the eagles
still sitting in their eyes; and would you look at the flaming
lass with the starshine on her and the dew, the bright morn-
ing to remind them of their midnight. . . Faith, Paddy, I'm
thinking there must be more to life than a road toward dying,
or nobody would ever agree to be born!

The scene reached its climax with dramatic suddenness.
After ceremonial overtures with calumet smoke, Chief Shegud
gave an impassioned oration. In reply Mrs. John Johnston,
Daughter of the Green Glade, spoke the words that stopped
the war drums:

"Listen to me! My face also is carved with sorrow because our ancient burial ground is violated. My brother
speaks straight. The land was given to us for as long as
grass grows and water flows. But those are old words, and
these are new times. Does my brother ask the sun to stand
still?

"Listen to me! My brother is too wise to heed the angry
counsels of young men. My brother knows that young men
are forever wanting to make war—or to make love.

"Listen to me! We have the legend of a mighty hero named
Manabozho who was sent to clear our rivers and open our
lakes. My brother remembers that Manabozho sailed into
the sunset before he tamed the white horses of St. Mary's
Falls.

"Listen to me! Now the palefaces have sent someone to
this place. He is not mighty Manabozho. He cannot scoop
up sandbars with his hands and hurl islands and boulders
from the rapids. He must have the help of many servants and
many kegs of thunder powder to dig his way around such
waterfalls as Manabozho would stamp down with his foot.

"Listen to me! Let us glory in the fact that from our an-
cestral bones will come new life for a continent. Let us take

pride that the gateway into Gitchee Gumee, the Big Sea Water, will be built through Indian graves——"

As Susan Marie picked the final words from her great-grandmother's lips and translated them for history, her eyes were brighter than wet paint. After a long look at Chief Shegud, the elderly woman in calico and deerhide took the girl's hand and moved away. The hushed crowd flowed aside. Captain Ringgold, then Harvey, lifted their beaver hats as she passed, and all along the line men bared their heads to an Ojibway princess.

2

Shotgun Wedding Threat

Leather-lunged commands from two-fisted foremen sent the canal gangs back into the big ditch to blast and shovel and wheel and sweat out the rest of the July day. Harvey, the Indian scare behind him, called a meeting of his staff in the shack that served as canal headquarters.

"Get this straight," said Harvey. "I have set my face like a flint to build this canal, and nothing short of death can stop me. I'll marry Lake Superior to the Lower Lakes, if I have to stage a shotgun wedding. And—make no mistake: I'll boss the works, I'll run the show, you'll take orders from nobody but me." His fists hammered the desk. "I'm the Soo Canal!"

"You're the white man's Manabozho," grinned Ringgold disarmingly. "Keep your shirt on and tell us what's biting you."

Harvey explained his flare of temper. Michigan had sent up a couple of state engineers to prepare the official survey, to chart the waters at the pier entrance to Lake Superior, to plan the locks and cofferdams, to inspect and to approve all canal progress.

"Major Glenn minds his business," granted Harvey, "but Colonel Canfield is an incompetent political appointee, all brass and no brains." He turned to excavation straw boss Chapel and to Nichols, engineering veteran of the Erie Canal. "My compliments to Colonel Canfield, and tell him to remove his swinging derricks from the cut . . . . Meeting adjourned!"

Ringgold stayed behind to present his cargo report; the number of kegs of Delaware blasting powder, heads of Kentucky jacks, barrels of Cincinnati pork, feet of special timber. "Also organized a fleet of twenty-five schooners to haul prime stone for the canal locks up from Malden and Sandusky, and——"

A gaunt man bristled into the office. His sunken cheeks were flagged with anger and he held himself corset-stiff. "Explain yourself, Harvey! I demand to know why you ordered my swinging derricks removed!"

Harvey studied the figures on his desk. "Because my excavation has proved twice as effective at only half the cost of yours, Colonel. I've also shelved your plans for the lock chamber floors and, instead of the old-fashioned lock gates you suggested, I'm getting the newest and best. Furthermore, although it's not demanded by contract as you've pointed out, I intend to trim up the jagged sides of the ditch and face any rough rock with Drummond Island limestone."

While the state engineer stared speechless, Harvey rapped out his policy. "I'll drive hard bargains, sir, but I won't build a second-rate canal."

"Why, you upstart traveling salesman——" Rigid with rage, Colonel Canfield checked himself and turned on his heel.

From the window, Ringgold watched his brittle progress along the canal cut. "There goes one with death in his face," he told Harvey. "That man won't live out the year. But his ghost might come back to haunt you!"

"Let's hope his ghost knows more about engineering than he does!" Harvey laughed, then threw a comradely arm around Ringgold. "You're staying with me at Elmwood, of course. There'll be whitefish for supper, and for sweet dreams a bed that Schoolcraft slept in. But don't get used to life ashore, not until ice locks up the lakes. . . ."

Ringgold learned the reason for that warning the next day when they toured the diggings. "We're running out of men," Harvey said savagely. "Railroad contractors send agents up here to offer them more money, the mine-owners bribe them from under our noses, the weather and the wilderness scare them away, and we've always got Slater and the Trowbridge faction to outsmart."

Harvey scowled at the dwindled gangs in the cut. "I want sixteen hundred shovels in that ditch before autumn, and next year I'll want double that many. I'm putting up thirty more shanties, I'm sending out a dozen more timber crews, I'm expanding the Drummond quarry, I'm building another barge fleet————"

"And you need bohunk carpenters and Scotch stun-hammers men, Androscoggin lumberjacks and Missouri mule-skinners, squarehead blacksmiths and Cornish powder monkeys and Scandihoovian hand-drill teams and Canadian chariot drivers, and every mother's son of Saint Patrick to put heart in the whole boiling kettle."

"Correct, Mr. Trouble Shooter," Harvey clapped Ringgold's shoulder. "I don't care how you get them, but—keep me supplied!"

"Count on it," Ringgold tall-talked. "I'll hire agents to board every immigrant ship before it docks in Boston or Philadelphia or New York, and tell the passengers there are diamonds for the diggings in this ditch. With Patrick Flynn I'll scour the lakes, sweep out the dives, comb the jails and loony bins. We'll hornswoggle, bamboozle, or shanghai anything in pants." Ringgold's voice sobered. "And no matter how we get them, they'll brag to their grandchildren about how they helped build the Soo Canal!"

3

A STOWAWAY ABOARD

Within the hour the *Huron Belle* chunked her paddle
wheels down the St. Mary's on a hunt for Old-Country and
New-State men. But Captain Ringgold soon met an international problem in one small package of personality. He
discovered a stowaway when he made landing at Paradise
Bay on Big Beaver Island in Lake Michigan to fuel up with
cordwood and to make arrangements for more mules with
King Strang who had a reputation of collecting the best looking women and the hardest working mules on the Lakes.

Susan Marie was caught as she stole out from under a deck
tarpaulin to peek at the Mormon leader. When he left the
boat, she blurted out her disappointment:

"He wasn't even wearing a crown! Does he really have a
wife for every day in the week?"

"You'll be sent back to the Soo on the first upbound boat
we hail," Ringgold scolded. "Even a very young lady can't
travel unchaperoned."

She tossed her red hairbows. "That is why I have per-
suaded my godfather to make the trip."

Ringgold investigated below. *Voila!* Hyacinth Beauharnais, gaudy-sashed and eagle-feathered, teaching Patrick
Flynn and his firemen how to play an old *voyageur* game on
a drumhead of Algoma cheese. Ah, *mes amis,* his fingers had
lost all cunning and surely their sharp eyes could tell under
which moccasin lay the lucky stone, but, to sweeten their
interest, he might risk a *picayune* wager. . . .

By the time the *Huron Belle* coasted down Lake Michigan
to log Milwaukee, Hyacinthe Beauharnais had money spilling
out of his ears, and Patrick Flynn had discovered the best
system to lure his countrymen into signing up for work at the
Soo!

"This way, boys! Free passage to the fights!"

Once aboard the *Huron Belle,* the future canallers were kept happy. Pat's jug never ran dry and the sailing songs they learned to while away the voyage all promised good times to come.

> *Oh, we didn't tarry-oh,*
> *On the blue Ontario,*
> *We were sailing to get ashore.*
> *So we blew across the lake*
> *With a wiggle and a shake,*
> *Far away from Niagara's roar.*
> *Got the captain's billy-goat*
> *When we jumped his silly boat*
> *At the head of the great St. Lawr.*
> *But it only took a day*
> *To blow in all our pay,*
> *So we shipped right back once more.*

"Now altogither on the chorus," Patrick Flynn would roar, carried away by song and Rumbellion combined. "And hit the big OH! with a bang!"

> *Oh, we will not tarry-oh,*
> *On the blue Ontario-OH!*
> *We're just sailing to get ashore.*

There were other ballads to match. They sang of land-lubbers who got "skeery" of stormy Lake Erie, and then a whole lot "skeerier" of stormy Lake Superior. Hyacinthe Beauharnais interrupted his old *voyageur* game long enough to teach everyone aboard ship the French dialect song long a favorite on the inland seas.

> *On wan dark night on Lak' San Clair,*
> *De win' she blow, blow, blow,*
> *An' de crew of de wood scow* Julie Plante
> *Got scair an' run below,*
> *For de win' she blow lak' hurricane,*
> *Bimeby she blow some more,*
> *An' de scow bus' up on Lak' San Clair,*
> *Ten acre from de shore.*

When the sun was shining and the waters were calm, the song the future canallers liked best had a catchy tune and a promise of rollicking times ahead at Sault Ste. Marie.

> *Oh, it's a so-long to Saginaw,*
> *And glad-to-meet-you Mackinaw;*
> *Lake Huron, we're sure on to you.*
> *You blew and swore to beat us,*
> *But we've got the steam to treat us*
> *To a glass and a lass at the Soo!*

But when the skies were black and the waves smashed against the *Huron Belle,* then sailors and passengers alike drew together and joined their voices in an old *revival hymn* that not only prayed for help but also represented the deep underlying spirit of these rough-hewn men who had given up their homes and security to put whatever strength and faith they possessed into the building of a canal for the future.

> *The* Gospel *Ship is now a-sailing*
> *Bound for* Canaan's *happy shore.*
> *All who wish to sail for* Glory,
> *Come and join us, rich and poor.*

As they sang, the *Huron Belle* made the grand circuit of Michigan's Mitten, or *sailed around the horseshoe,* as Lakemen more commonly called it. With one prong at Chicago and the other at Buffalo, the Michigan Horseshoe had the top of its arc at the Straits of Mackinac, and it was a good-luck charm for commerce and navigation from the Eastern to the Western states, and back again.

Susan Marie pestered Ringgold's long watches at the wheel. Later, he would remember where the *Huron Belle* had been when the girl said this or that, and so he could chart it in his mind, but all he could pin down was the geography—not the quicksilver of her thoughts. They were off Sleeping Bear along Grand Traverse Bay, for instance, when she turned abruptly and told him:

"I am not so young. I have seventeen years, and I count time by the beat of my heart, not by the tick-tick of a clock!"

Mackinac Island glowed like an emerald in the side-wheeler's wake when she decided aloud to transfer her affections to young Doctor Jessup at the Canal Company Hospital on Rapids Island. "It is always good business to have a doctor in the family," she said.

As the *Huron Belle* breasted Windmill Point and went sweethearting down the Detroit River, Susan Marie showed Ringgold an ermine charm bag fashioned for her by Hyacinthe Beauharnais. There were Isle Royale sparkle-tones in a nest of sweet grass, but the most important charm——

"Look! I carry the claws of a crab. Because the crab has claws that hold very tightly and this means that I will hold on to everything I like. You see?" She said this in a fierce little sing-song, as if she were trying to convince herself, as well as him. "One must have faith," she told Ringgold. "Me, I am a great believer in crab claws!"

On Lake Erie within sight of Put-in-Bay, she screwed up her mouth to admit that Genesee Trowbridge was attractive. "But you only think you love her," said Susan Marie. "You are really in love with five sisters, and all of them are great ladies, but every one of them is a sweet-water sea. This is a topsy-turvy, wrong-way-around world," she sighed a heart-beat later. "You want her, she wants Mr. Harvey, and I am your little sister!"

Twenty knots from Buffalo, she came out of a spell of brooding to bring up the time Cole Slater had called her a breed. "It is true," she said, a tiny catch in her voice. "But I am proud of my blood."

Captain Eureka Longfellow Ringgold steadied the wheel and swept Susan Marie into the harbor of one brawny arm. "Your mother was an Eldridge from the North of England and your grandmother was a Beaufait of Montreal. Your great-aunt Jane was Henry Schoolcraft's wife. Your great-grandfather was an Irish nobleman and your great-grand-mother is an Ojibway princess. With a pedigree like that, you can turn up your nose and spit in anybody's eye!"

As she tried to twist away from his kindness, he pinned her tighter. "You don't know how lucky you are," he said. "Some of us have to invent families." While she listened in rosy wonder, he told her how the steamer *James Monroe* went down during a Lake Ontario storm, how Dad Ringgold's schooner *Pretty Kate* picked up a baby in a cradle lashed to a makeshift raft, how the orphan was named Eureka to sig-nify a foundling. As the years sailed him toward manhood, the boy learned the lore of the lakes firsthand, but Dad Ring-gold also insisted on shore schooling, and so Eureka was in an Ann Arbor classroom when word came that the *Pretty Kate* had been swallowed with all hands on Green Bay the howling November before the Mexican War. He had joined the First Michigan Regiment under Colonel McReynolds and was decorated twice on the road from Vera Cruz to Chapul-tepec, but he would rather have had one of his comrade's letters from home than all the medals on General Scott's chest. When mail call came around he felt so alone in the world that he invented the Pennsylvania branch of the Long-fellow family and claimed a poet for cousin. Not knowing any real relatives, he picked his favorite author.

"I never expected an answer to my first letter, and when he wrote I showed it to the whole army. Fact is, I began to more than half believe my own lies—" Ringgold scowled suddenly. "So don't get any foolish ideas about your blood, and if you ever tell anyone what I've just told you, I'll shave your head and paint it for an Easter egg!"

After his talk with Susan Marie, Ringgold's conscience nudged him to reveal the deception to Longfellow. A man could not go forever living a lie. Besides, what was the sense of keeping a poet for a cousin if he wouldn't write so much as a sonnet about Lake Superior?

4

Mr. Longfellow Says *No*

In his Cambridge study a Harvard professor sat at a desk that seemed to have been struck by an avalanche of books and papers. Amid this tranquil chaos, Longfellow read Ringgold's letter. His eyes twinkled and his beard twitched in the process, but the reply he sent to Sault Ste. Marie reflected depths of understanding beneath the bantering surface words, depths that showed why the fates had singled him out as a poet:

> DEAR COUSIN RINGGOLD: I have your so-called confession at hand, and I feel that youth and lack of logic have led you to rash conclusions. Since you don't know who you are, Coz, how dare you assume you aren't a Longfellow? Can you prove there isn't a Pennsylvania branch of the family, and that you aren't a member of it? Until you produce such proof, Coz, I refuse to be disinherited. I admire the idea of having a cousin who is tub-thumper for a wilderness, psalm-singer for Lake Superior, troubadour for a backwoods canal. And, by the way, Coz, I haven't forgotten your request for a few verses booming the Northwest in Horatian (Greeley) style. At this moment I am surrounded by the Schoolcraft volumes you sent me, and I hope in due season to present you with a souvenir. Meanwhile, I beg to remain — at least until I receive better evidence to the contrary — your cousin,
>
> *Henry Wadsworth Longfellow*

5

A Bonny Widow Applies

The letter arrived at the Soo the same week the *Huron Belle* docked below the rapids that blocked ship passage into Lake Superior. Ringgold reported immediately to Canal Headquarters.

"We packed so many canallers aboard that Pat Flynn will have to pry them off with a crowbar, and there's more coming," he told Harvey. "We've got slick-tongued agents with fast-talking dollars in every port from here to Hoboken, and I've offered a bonus to all lake captains for quick delivery." His voice lost momentum as he noticed Harvey's battered knuckles. "What have I missed?"

"We had a cholera scare, but Doctor Jessup diagnosed the the trouble as bad whisky." Harvey flexed his broad shoulders. "Which gives me an excuse to break up those grogshops on wheels that Slater talked the bartenders into operating along the canal cut."

Ringgold sighed. "I still don't care for your teetotal opinions, but I do like the look of your fists . . . . Any other excitement?"

"A heavy toll in accidents. Blasting through Cambrian sandstone isn't the best guarantee of old age. I've worked out a hospitalization plan for the men—twenty-five cents deducted from each pay check sees them through any sickness or crippling injury— but that's no protection against violent death. I'm cracking down on carelessness, too, but some of the accidents have the shape of design, although I haven't been able to trace them directly to Slater or Trowbridge."

"What about Colonel Canfield?"

"Won't communicate with me except through his assistant, Major Glenn," Harvey chuckled. "He finished the official canal survey and charted the waters at the Lake Superior pier entrance far ahead of schedule. Now he's puttering around with plans for a cofferdam that ought to keep him off my neck until next year."

"How many more toes have you stepped on since I left?"

"Let's see—" Harvey considered. "I ordered Doctor Musgrave not to peddle any of his quack prescriptions on canal property; I booted fat Philo Worts out of the office when he tried to rent me a warehouse for triple its value; and I accused Publisher Bisby in public of being short in his land-office accounts. The three of them have joined Slater and Trowbridge in a sort of barroom cabal. They meet at the Golden Fleece and hatch devilment against the canal works. The last issue of the *Soo Sentinel* called me an unlicked cub and nicknamed the ditch Harvey's Folly!"

Ringgold half turned. "You've a knack for making the right kind of enemies," he grinned. "Now let's see how fast you can make a friend. I've brought a lady to see you. Michael Phelan's widow is waiting to ask you about a job as cook. I've got a hunch she's a good-luck piece—"

"Wait a minute!" Harvey howled.

Outside in the waiting room, Ringgold bowed. "Go right in, Mrs. Phelan, and don't mind his bark. He'll be delighted to see you."

Pleasant, plump, and on the sunny side of thirty, she bounced into Harvey's office with three little girls tagging at her heels. They were neat as needles, scrubbed to the bone, and they all bobbed a curtsy and looked at him as if he were about to hand them the pot of gold at the rainbow's end.

Harvey avoided their eyes. He had no job for an immigrant widow with three children ranging from four to ten. His commissary system housed fifty men to each shanty with a strong-armed couple in charge, to provide food and clean berths for the gang, and to maintain order. To put a small sized widow and three tiny images among fifty roughnecks would be inviting disaster. In justice to herself and her family, Harvey explained, he would have to refuse.

None of the four shiny faces lost that look of good news coming. The widow turned and smiled at the children. Three small daughters beamed back at Mama. They all knew a wonderful secret. And, as a prelude of letting the canal boss in on it, the widow gave a decisive poke at her bonnet.

"Sure, and you could never refuse to hire the widow of
Michael Phelan, peace to his memory," she proclaimed with
ringing confidence. "Him as was respected by great men in
the old country and, if it's proof you're wanting, here's a certificate from Lord John Russell himself that tells about his
fine character." As if she were passing a prayer book in
church, she handed Harvey a sheet of paper:

> Estates of Lord J. Russell, County Clare, Ireland, October
> 12, 1852. To Michael Phelan: You are hereby notified to
> vacate the earth-walled thatched tenement now occupied
> by yourself and family near the Dublin Road, within
> thirty days of receipt hereof, as it is to be torn down and
> removed, by order of his lordship,
>
> *Attest, Shaun Fogarty, Agent for said Estates*

Harvey glanced from the paper to the widow. He saw a
guileless woman who obviously could not read. Perhaps the
husband who had died en route to America had misrepre-
sented the letter to her, perhaps someone else had played the
trick. That was unimportant. What counted was the glow
on those four faces, the faith in a husband and father whom
Lord Russell—so they believed—had written about for all
the world to see.

"You are right, Mrs. Phelan," said Harvey, returning the
letter with studied care. "That recommendation settles all
arguments. The Soo Canal cannot refuse a job to the widow
of Michael Phelan. There's an opening for a cook in Shanty
Twenty-five."

Down went the precious document into the place nearest
the widow's heart. Triumphantly she nodded to her three
little girls. Back to Mama came three I-told-you-so nods.
None of them had felt a moment's doubt. Good news coming!

When Harvey called for a volunteer to maintain order in
Shanty Number Twenty-five, every Irishman in the diggings
stepped forward, but Patrick Flynn beat them all to the care-
taker's door, where he held the fort with one eye on Michael

Phelan's widow and the other eye on the applewood shille-
lagh in his fist. "It's sad I am to be deserting you and the
Huron Belle," he told Ringgold, "but, faith, and I see now
there's more important work for a man right here, and my
duty lies clear and sweet before me."

At the end of the widow's first week, rumors of a fabulous
hash swept the diggings. Chief Steward Norman Day's desk
was flooded with applications for transfer to Number Twenty-
five. Regular inmates of the shanty were envied as darlings
of fortune. As for the roughnecks Harvey had feared might
cause disorder—

When the widow sailed for Mission Church on Sunday
with her three small craft in tow, all fifty of her crew followed at a respectful distance. They were glad-ragged in canal
finery, some of them had plug hats clapped over their cow-
licks, others twirled gold-knobbed canes in their calloused
paws, and the whole brawny shebang dared anyone to so
much as spit in the path of her dainty shoes, for the most
conspicuous objects they wore were the hearts on their sleeves.

Harvey, fighting time as cold weather approached, offered
seats at the widow's table to each week's fastest drill team.
Three stalwarts to a team, they swung sledges and drove
steel, poured powder into the hole and tamped it down. The
teams loosed hurricanes of rock in Harvey's ditch, and
dreamed of the widow's hash.

6

SHOOTING THE RAPIDS

Although he begrudged any time spent away from the job,
Harvey realized the value of entertaining famous visitors who
might take back good reports to the Canal Company directors.
The most distinguished guests of the season were ex-President
Fillmore and his twenty-one-year-old daughter Mary Abigail

who inspected the canal works and enjoyed a stay at Elmwood.

Highlight of the visit was an outing over the Falls of St.
Mary's. After one glance at the raging white water, Mr.
Fillmore had declined.

"No doubt a thrilling experience," he said dryly, "but I
think I can live without it. You go along, if you want to run
the risk, Mary Abigail."

There were other polite refusals, and what began as a large
party finally dwindled down to three young couples placed in
separate canoes with Indian guides hired by Harvey. With
thoughtless disregard of possible preferences, he himself
squired Mary Abigail, put Genesee with Ringgold, and Susan
Marie with trim Dr. Jessup. This arrangement pleased the
ex-president's daughter, but Genesee's eyes were on Harvey's
canoe and Susan Marie never took hers off Ringgold's as Ojibway paddles dipped into the swift current.

"Let's go!" Harvey told the guides. "Shoot the rapids!"

The three girls screamed in excitement as the canoes hit
the point of no-return. Down they went in the frail birch-
barks, down with a whirl and a splash, through the hissing,
roaring, rock-throated maelstrom, like Jonah swallowed by
the whale, for seven spray-drenched minutes of twists and
turns and tosses until they were spumed out on the broad
bosom of the St. Mary's more than a mile below, all of them
dizzy as the swirling rapids themselves.

Slowly the canoes drifted together. "Now I understand
how wise you are, sir," Miss Fillmore half-joked to Harvey.
"I see you are taking the advice of Mrs. Jameson in building
your canal. She wrote in her *Travels* that these rapids must
be treated the way a man treats a beautiful passionate woman
—he does not oppose her, for that would be madness—but
he gets *round* her!"

"Oh?" said Genesee in such a flat voice and with such a
pointed stare at Harvey that Miss Fillmore guessed an open

secret known apparently to everyone but the former traveling salesman.

"We better start back," Ringgold said hastily. "There's a
chill on this water and the ladies might catch cold. Don't you
think so, Doctor Jessup?"

The young doctor, entranced by Susan Marie, failed to
hear the question, but she had an answer on the tip of her
saucy tongue. "Me, I feel warm but I suppose people with
Esquimaux blood always feel a chill."

That was the end of the last social affair of the season at
the Soo. From then on, without a pause except for Sunday,
Harvey drove his bog-trotting Irish along the line of a ditch
scheduled to wind up exactly one hundred and twenty feet
longer than a mile. Never mind the locks and the piers now;
that would come later. First he had to make his mile and a
little more, a hundred feet wide and twelve feet deep, arc-
ing around St. Mary's Falls, the start of a national pike where
freighters of fortune could ply back and forth with the wealth
of a continent and cargoes for the world. But no use dreaming about that until five thousand four hundred feet of almost
solid Cambrian sandstone all the way, twice as deep as two
tall men, wider than a Parisian boulevard, had been chan-
neled out—until untold tons of flinty rock had been drilled,
blasted, shoveled, wheelbarrowed, and mule-carted to the
dump—until the dump became a mountain range of rubble
for the housewives of the Soo to shade their eyes at and declare:

"That crazy Harvey!"

He *was* a little mad, said Ringgold. He had to be for a
finish fight with that country. Even the mouse-colored pony
he rode along the diggings had a mad gleam in her eye. Left
saddled by Harvey while he supervised the touching off of
heavy blasts in the cut, she learned to scramble out of danger
with the canallers and return only after the shower of rocks

had ended. Her hide had been peppered and pockmarked
with flying stones, but, like her master, she always came back
for more.

Powder-blackened jaws clamped down as strong teeth bit
copper caps to fuses. The canal gangs jumped when the boss
hollered. They blasted the squares off the calendar, they
wheelbarrowed the weeks away with the rubble, and there
weren't enough hours in the day for Harvey.

The men were sure that he never went to bed. They saw
him first thing in the morning, last thing at night. The Irish
said that he walked in his sleep and sighted his level by the
glow of the *aurora borealis.* They could tell by the signs in
the frost on the ground, come ivery dawn, whispered the
Irish, and although Himself had brogans smaller than most,
sure and he left the biggest tracks of all behind him . . . .

With the skies turning to slate and ice cakes tossing in
the Rapids, the Soo began to live up to its nickname of Michigan's Siberia. Ringgold joined the oldtimer's in putting on
a second shirt. When the real cold came they would put on
another and call it three-shirt weather.

7

SECOND THESSALONIANS, III, 10

A week before the first blizzard, Michael Phelan's widow
sought out Harvey in great distress. The struggle between
loyalty to him and love for the men showed on her troubled
face. She blurted out her story: a strike, instigated by Slater's
ringleaders, was brewing. Her hands twisted uneasily in her
lap.

"Get yourself and your little girls to Elmwood where they'll
be safe," said Harvey. He meant to meet this his favorite
way, headlong, slam-bang, no quarter asked or given. At
ten o'clock the next morning when the gangs threw down
their tools and swarmed out of the cut toward the Soo's bars

and bowling alleys, he turned to Ringgold and said: "What's your idea, Mr. Trouble Shooter?"

"New Testament, Second Thessalonians, Chapter Three, Verse Ten," Ringgold said cryptically. "St. Paul had the right answer to this problem."

Harvey looked up his Bible and called a council of war. He issued crisp orders to foremen and shanty caretakers. Ringgold passed out shotguns and Patrick Flynn distributed applewood shillelaghs. While the canal gangs were on a holiday spree, mule teams hauled supply wagons laden with provisions into the woods, where the stores of food were hidden.

Supper time came. The men returned to their shanties for steaming bowls of Irish potatoes and sizzling platters of fried whitefish and scalding mugs of tea.

Harvey's reception committees met them, pointing to crude signs over the doorposts: NO WORK, NO GRUB! The strikers pushed inside to gape at bare tables, empty shelves, gutted cupboards. They came out, hot-eyed and empty-bellied, hard-fisted and full of fight. The tramp of their brogans thundered like buffalo down a canyon.

From the porch at Canal Headquarters, Harvey and Ringgold faced that charge of seventeen hundred tough-fibered men. "I'll make no bargains," Harvey roared. "The town can't feed you, and there's no boat out until spring. You'll go to bed hungry tonight, and you'll wake up hungrier tomorrow, and you'll dig my ditch or you'll starve!"

The mob surged forward as Slater's ringleaders yelled: "We'll manhandle them into telling us where they stowed the food! Rush 'em, boys! Smash the works!"

That was a time for Michael Phelan's widow to poke her bonny head out an upstairs window and cry: "Would you listen to me now, you spalpeens, or have you lost all taste for a dish of hash?"

Hash! They stopped in their tracks. They mooned up at
the widow, their mouths watering. Sure, and she looked
good enough to eat herself, but her hash—heaven on a plate!

"If you'll go back to work in the morning, with no more
foolishness," she said, "I'll sweep the floor of every shanty
kitchen come Saturday and make hash for the whole camp!
And that's a bargain I'll keep with you every week of the
world until you've finished the job for Mr. Harvey," promised
Michael Phelan's widow. "Are you with me or against me?"

Their answer reverberated to the top of Canada. Hash
every Saturday for all the shanty boys! The widow knew the
way to their hearts.

"I had a hunch," Ringgold reminded Harvey, "she'd be a
good-luck piece."

8

CARCAJOU WINTER

Overnight, winter blew in from Hudson Bay. The *Huron
Belle* froze at her moorings, ice-locked for six months to come.
Ringgold moved ashore into Elmwood to help Harvey scheme
how to beat the great white cold. They figured out a system of
huge bonfires along the diggings, they stationed watchers
on the wheelbarrow runways to spot the telltale frostbite at
the tip of a man's nose, to scour his face with snow, to shove
him toward a bonfire. With Indian summer long gone,
Squaw winter screamed at the Soo. The mercury lost the
habit of rising above zero. Sides of beef hung outside the
Canal kitchens froze stiffer than planks, and shanty cooks
hacked off what they needed with their axes.

Ringgold taught Harvey a Lake Superior trick to make
himself tougher than any of his men. "I'll show you how,"
he said one morning at dawn, getting ready to suit his actions
to his words. "If you're out of your mind too, you can follow

my example. Ready? Okay. Throw off your warm covers, like this—Jump out of bed onto the cold floor in your bare feet, like this—Run outside and dive into the nearest snowbank like this—Yow! Roll around in the stuff for a minute and yell like you were being murdered, which we probably are—Hustle back inside, throw a log on the fire, rub yourself down with a rough towel, and hope you'll thaw out in time for breakfast."

It was a kill-or-cure treatment, but they both were built to survive. In the case of the canal gangs, however, not a week passed without its deaths to record. Men went mad working in a white jungle and a glare of ice. Slyly they wandered away from the bonfires into the savage smother of the wooly-whippers lashing down from the Arctic Circle.

They tossed aside their picks and shovels and, wearing secret smiles, walked into the staggering blasts and out of the world. Many of the bodies would not be discovered until first thaw. The Irish crossed themselves and, borrowing a Canadian superstition, muttered that their mates had heard the howling of a loupgarou in the voice of the storm. They mentioned other names in hushed tones: Banshee, Lorelei, and Michigan's own Carcajou, the Fiendish Wolverine, the wisest and most wicked of all.

Some canallers drank heavily to forget the winter, but there was danger in this escape. Drunks, lurching from the grog shops at midnight, were found the next morning frozen into weird attitudes, carved into statues by the cold.

The men in the cut grumbled that the dead were the lucky ones. It was raw, murderous work for those who remained on the job. There were days when the earth and sky and air were churned into a strangling chaos; when the sleet drew blood from their faces, ripping into them like rocksalt from a shotgun; treacherous bright clear days when the paralyzing cold pounced from ambush. But Harvey drove his canal gangs, and himself, through them all.

Over hot buttered rum in the Golden Fleece, the barroom cabal made plans for Harvey's downfall. In its weekly issues the *Soo Sentinel* carried unfavorable reports of canal progress and predictions of failure.

In his struggle with the elements, Harvey forgot that a printing press can blow more damage than any storm. He laughed at the paper, and Publisher Bisby bared his teeth like a mule eating thistles, because every time the Ojibway mailman plodded down the Snowshoe Pike toward civilization, he toted copies of the *Soo Sentinel* addressed to all the directors of the St. Mary's Falls Ship Canal Company as well as to the key newspapers in Detroit and New York.

With winter mail deliveries slow and uncertain, the canal opposition figured it would be weeks, possibly months, before this attack against Harvey produced any results. Meanwhile, they kept their heads together, scheming ways and means to halt or delay the progress of the work.

Ringgold stomped into the office with the first bad news. "They've bought that swampland between town and the timber sections," he reported to Harvey one below-zero noon. "And they've put up no-trespassing signs at each end of the road where it crossed their land. Legally, you can't use that road anymore."

Harvey showed his teeth. "I built the road. I need the timber. Tell the sled teamsters and the lumberjacks to tear down those signs. Keep that cordwood coming. I want these bonfires blazing sky-high along the cut, and plenty of timber for shoring, and logs for cookstoves." He pushed out his jaw. "And here's what you can tell those trouble-makers—"

What Ringgold relayed to them blistered their ears. They retaliated by serving legal documents on Harvey. He tore them up and threw the scraps in their faces. They threatened to prosecute him, and he thumbed his nose.

"Sue me next summer when Judge Goodwin makes his rounds," he taunted them. "Right now I'm the law on this canal!"

That night Cole Slater came back from across the frozen St. Mary's River, leading a rum-soaked band of Canucks who chopped down trees and blocked the timber road, then reeled back to the Canadian side of the Soo to drink the rest of their night's hire.

In the morning, Harvey hitched the mouse-colored pony to a red sleigh and drove out to inspect the mischief. "Clear out the obstruction," he ordered his woods crew, hoisting the butt end of a felled tree himself. "How long will it take these people to learn that nobody can stop progress?"

The cabal grew bolder. Slater ordered his French Canadians to block the timber road by daylight, and in jig-time Harvey's red sleigh blew into the Canal Company's wood camp on a back trail. Soon afterwards the tipsy Canucks heard ominous sounds in the distance.

Around a bend in the road suddenly appeared a lumberjack corps marching in military style, with axes on shoulders in place of muskets, and with an enormous Irishman beating a large copper-country kettle to make up for a brass band.

"Jump, ye frog-eaters!" yelled Patrick Flynn. "Jump for the far shore or we'll climb down your throats and tear out your wishbones for fun!"

The battle royal began with the healthy thump of fists and ended with the thud of boots as Harvey's lumberjacks tried to speed the Canucks on their way with parting kicks. Slater's hirelings took to their heels like deer whiteflagging through brush, and were last seen as they darted behind the Hudson's Bay Post.

"Quick as you tap a man's claret, he loses whatever Dutch courage he's taken aboard," Ringgold commented, giving a technical explanation somewhat obscure to a boss whose strongest drink was raspberry shrub.

"I don't think they'll try that trick again," Harvey said, "but I wish I knew what those diehards were going to pull out of their sleeves next."

"Expect the worst," Ringgold said, "and nobody'll be disappointed!"

9

SNOWSHOE PIKE—WALL STREET

The Soo laughed as heartily at the Canuck stampede as it had laughed at the time Patrick Flynn took Michael Phalen's widow on a fishing trip of a Sunday, breaking his back to chop a hole through four feet of ice in the St. Mary's River before he could lower a line, and then—"It's cold I am," said the widow, "would you be taking me back now?"

But the last laugh of the winter was enjoyed by the barroom cabal at Harvey's expense. Their system of blackmail finally paid dividends.

One morning at the height of bad weather, Ringgold stomped snow into Canal Headquarters to give Harvey the daily trouble-shooting report. "About average," he said. "Forty below. Doc Jessup's treating about a hundred new cases of frostbite. Three more amputations. One drunk found frozen dead. Five more canallers missing, and probably won't be found until spring. Last night's snow buried a team of mules and hid a toolshed out of sight. Can't locate it anywhere."

Never noticing Harvey's long face and clenched jaws, Ringgold turned to more personal matters. "That spunky little rascal Susan Marie shot the timber wolf that's been gorging on the Soo's cattle. And I'm taking the afternoon off to bundle Genesee Trowbridge into a cutter and show her Whitefish Bay with the ice banked up for forty miles like giant windowpanes. You might as well tag along with us," Ringgold added a shade ruefully. "All she talks about is you."

"I'm building a canal, I've got no time for girls!" Harvey barked. "And neither have you!" He unclenched his fist, showing a crumpled letter. "This just came from the Board of Directors. Bisby mailed them copies of that collection of lies and gossip he calls a newspaper. They want explanations, fast! A letter wouldn't work and I can't spare myself from the job. You're elected! Head East and brace them up.

"Tell them not to believe the slanders in the *Sentinel*. Tell them to believe in the future. We're building for it here at the Soo. This isn't just a canal, it's a gateway to fortune. We'll move whole mountains of red iron ore over this ditch and sit the United States on top of the world. We'll carry enough copper through here to girdle the globe with telegraph wires and put a shiny bottom on every ship afloat. We'll haul the golden harvests from the breadbasket lands across the Soo, the grain from the Dakotas, and Manitoba and Saskatchewan."

Harvey's eyes held the glint of far horizons. "I'm talking big, but I'm talking to fit the country. This is just a start, we're scratching the surface, that's all. Why, steamboats the size of today—they could be stuck in the pockets of the liners that will be passing through the Soo tomorrow. But we're blazing the trail. They'll look back on us and they'll wonder that so few and so feeble a people working under so cold a sky should have accomplished so much for the world."

Harvey's voice trailed off and the vital force drained from his eyes. "Or maybe they won't think about us at all. But that's not important. Get back East and sell those directors a bill of goods to keep us going!"

"I'll sell them," said Ringgold, "or break something trying!"

Down the Snowshoe Pike he racqueted on bear-paw webs —sixty frozen miles to Mackinac Island, two hundred more through the pine barrens to semi-civilization at Saginaw, five shuffling days and four huddled nights on the trail—and he could have kissed the log-jammed Tittabawassee River when it came into view. *"Got a foot like a feather, a fist like a hammer—"* he sang.

By stageline and railroad, through the still reverberating Erie War, he streaked Eastward, where grave-faced directors had called a special meeting in New York to satisfy the shareholders and reach a decision about the unfavorable press reports copied by metropolitan papers from the *Soo Sentinel.* In a hickory shirt with rolled up sleeves Ringgold stood up against all their questions— even the one that brought a traveling salesman's rash promise home to roost:

"What about Harvey's four-hundred-thousand-dollar estimate to complete the canal? He's already spent that much of our money!"

"Your money!" snorted Ringgold. "I wouldn't brag about poor stuff that hides in a bank anytime somebody yells boo! You can take your money and—"

"Gentlemen, gentlemen!" Chairman Corning called for order.

Ringgold roared back. "We've spent sweat and blood and lives up there, and do you think Harvey would skimp on the job to fit his canal into a miserable budget? Stop whining about your cry-baby dollars. We want gangway into the greatest of inland seas, into a body of water so beautiful that God set it up on the roof of the world to keep ordinary eyes from spying on His Glory, into the Queen of Lakes that He created nineteen degrees colder than Hudson Bay to guard the treasures that she holds on her lap and wears in her copper crown—"

Thaddeus Fairbanks made signs for his brothers and for young Charles Hosmer Morse to draw closer to him at the conference table. "Listen to that," he whispered. "Must be something in the water up there at the Soo. They get touched

with it. Look what happened to Harvey. Maybe all the energy flowing through the rapids bounces and bubbles into their
blood. Wish we had a few bottles of it to put backbone in
this crowd!"

"Pretty words!" sneered a Wall Street manipulator in answer to Ringgold. "But let's be sensible, gentlemen. Face the
figures. At present rate of canal construction, the lands we
receive in payment will cost us more than a dollar an acre.
My friends, we could have purchased any amount of Michigan lands for ninety cents an acre. Consider the risk, gentlemen! *That canal must be completed in little more than a
year from now, or the lands are forfeit. In plain words, we
are placed in the impossible position of paying too much for
something we might not even get!*"

He polished his glasses to allow time for the argument to
sink in, then spread his hands in an age-old gesture. "Gentlemen, I suggest we withdraw from this deal, and—let's be
blunt—manipulate the market so the common shareholders
will cover our losses."

Erastus Fairbanks shot to his feet. "Sir," he thundered,
"consider yourself bought out, and use that door quickly before you're thrown out!"

Then he told the rest of them: "My brothers and I figure
what's good for the country will be good for our business.
That's why we're still backing the Soo Canal. Also," he added dryly, "we aim to see that it's completed on time. We op-
erate on the profit system and we're counting on collecting
the land grant from Michigan to get a reasonable return on
our investment. Without a canal at the Soo, the land beyond
will never be worth much. But, once a canal opens up commerce, who knows what the timber and iron and copper lands
may bring?"

History, dealing in futures, cocked an ear and chuckled,
marking time to prove that a salesman had picked land in

bonanza lots. But right now the calamity howlers were bolt-
ing for the door, sliding out of a deal that looked shaky,
squeezing their nickels.

In the hubbub, Thaddeus Fairbanks spoke to Charles Hosmer Morse. "Suppose you were an honest-to-Pete partner in
this firm, son," he said, "what would you advise me and my
brothers to do?"

Young Mr. Morse stroked his chin in a vain effort to look
older than twenty. He strove for a deep voice, but only
suceeded in making it sound as if he had caught cold. However, his suggestion went beyond his years.

"What everyone's been reading in the newspapers doesn't
count," he said. "I like the way Captain Ringgold talks, but
that doesn't count either. There's no sense in pinning any
belief on what we read or hear. This is a matter of business,
and *seeing* is believing."

Then with a rapid, "And that's my opinion for what it's
worth to Fairbanks and Company," young Mr. Morse stroked
fiercely at a beard that existed only in his own hopeful
imagination.

"You mean Fairbanks, *Morse* and Company, don't you,
son?" Thaddeus said, repeating his favorite bit of gentle
raillery that always had enough serious undertone to make
his brothers glance sharply at him and then stare at Charles
Hosmer Morse as if they were seeing their young accountant
for the first time.

"Well, boys, you just heard our junior partner," Thaddeus
went on in the same bantering style, and then his voice
changed abruptly. "Now let's call this conference to order
and get down to what we came here to do."

Ringgold, banished to another room while the directors
thrashed out a decision, waited for what seemed a glacial age
until they called him back into a meeting blue with smoke
and hard words. He stared anxiously at the three Fairbanks

brothers, who seemed beaten down and wilted with strain.

"Don't waste time on bad news," he said. "I won't take back word that doesn't give Harvey a fighting chance."

Thaddeus Fairbanks invented a wink to match his scales. "We had to fire half the Board of Directors, son, but we won you a breathing spell."

"You may tell Mr. Harvey," said President Corning of the New York Central, "that he has until June to produce satisfactory results. We'll appoint a committee to investigate the canal works at that time——"

BOOK FOUR

Ontario Ribbon

Up and down the river went they,
In and out among its islands,
Cleared its bed of root and sand-bar,
Dragged the dead trees from the channel,
Made its passage safe and certain,
Made a pathway for the people.

Song of Hiawatha

BOOK FOUR

Ontario Ribbon

1

Susan Marie Hears The Huntsmen

THE LAST DAY of June, traditional month of brides and battles, found the Soo abnormally calm for a paddle-and-portage outpost smack in the path of a mining boom and a canal war.

While he bossed the unloading of canal gates side-wheeled up the inland seas from Pittsburgh, Captain Ringgold watched the headwaters of civilization whiten with sails as a Lake Erie schooner fleet pulled in from the Marblehead quarries with flooring and walling for the locks. He bawled his orders into pandemonium that was music to his ears because it told the world how young Harvey's rumbling mile of big ditch had hit high gear in its race around the rapids toward Lake Superior.

Ringgold heard melodic overtones in the stomp and bray of mule teams, in the squeak and squeal of Irish wheelbarrows shuttling from cut to dump, in the chip and chisel of Scotch stun-hammers trimming blocks of limestone along the embankment, in the clamor of carpenters swarming on pier scaffolds and in the shrill of powder monkeys as they sang out, "Get going, boys, she's blowing!" before another blast of rock shook Sault Ste. Marie from American to Canadian shore.

No wonder, thought the young lakeman, that the Investigating Committee sent from New York by a panicky Board of Directors had given Harvey the go-ahead to continue the job after one whirlwind week of look-see at the canal works. Fresh in Ringgold's memory echoed Harvey's answer to the

Eastern expert who gaped at a new steeple etched against the wilderness skyline, then exclaimed:

"How in heaven's name did you find time to build that?"

"There's always time to build a church," said the twenty-five-year-old son of Reverend Joseph Harvey. "Or else it's too late to build anything."

Captain Ringgold grinned. A Connecticut Yankee who wouldn't take a drink or work a lick on Sunday was driving a canal across the roof of the world. It took all kinds to shape the future. . . .

At just that moment the most bewildering kind of all caught his eye. Susan Marie Beaufait Eldridge Johnston, on tiptoe among the dock watchers, almost waved her arm off at him and then, in answer to his call, came dancing from the crowd, her smile the biggest part of her.

"Stick right here until I'm finished with this job," he told her sternly. "I've got a bone to pick with you, young lady!"

His frown only brightened her smile, but at least it pinned her to the dock. Ever since spring she had been promenading the Soo with Doctor Jessup, and the sight rubbed Ringgold the wrong way. So, as soon as the canal gates were hoisted ashore, he walked her up Portage Avenue to the Falls of St. Mary's, where he spread his skipper coat on the grass, and talked to her like a Dutch uncle.

"Stop trying to act so grown-up," he lectured. "And what was wrong with your hair in braids? Why pile it up on your head like a lump of coal?"

"Because," Susan Marie squiggled her nose, "Doctor Jessup likes it this way."

"Oh, he does, does he?" Ringgold tore up a fistful of grass. "I wouldn't trust him too far, little sister. When a man grows a mustache, he's generally got something to hide."

"Me, I find it most enchanting, that mustache," she said. "And how does your own romance march with Miss Trowbridge? I wouldn't trust her very far either," mimicked Susan Marie. "Not the way she looks at Mr. Harvey!"

"Hush that talk," he growled. "Wild little Indian!"

"True for you," she agreed in shanty lingo. "In Ojibway I am named Sunbeams Breaking Through Clouds. My grandfather used to call me that, and he was a wild Irish Indian, which is the wildest kind of all. Me, I am very much like him. I can even hear the talk of the *Mist People,* the way he could—listen." She paused, but all Ringgold could hear was the sound of Lake Superior spilling over the Falls of St. Mary's.

"Under the roar and rumble you must listen for them," said Susan Marie. "They are faint, but clear, the *Voices of the Rapids.* The *voyageurs* call them the *Huntsmen,* and sometimes, if you listen close, they foretell the future. Today they are singing the boat song—*Vole, mon coeur, vole!* At least," she added suddenly shy, "it is what I think they are singing. My grandfather once told me that we hear only what is in our hearts."

Solemn for an instant, the girl closed her eyes and bent her head toward the falls. "Trouble upstream, the *Huntsmen* say. They are calling: 'Faster, faster! *Vole, mon coeur, vole!*'" Her mood somersaulted. "I think maybe it is time for me to go home and peel the potatoes," she said, and was up and away in a swish and foam of skirts.

Hyacinthe Beauharnais, smoking a long Quebec pipe on the Johnston veranda, saw her come flying up the lane, and the *voyageur* blood in his ancient veins sang like sparkling Burgundy. Then her arms were around him and her breath blew sweet and warm in his ear:

"Godfather! It begins to work, I hope and believe!"

She pirouetted, and from its hiding place drew the tiny charm bag he had fashioned for her from ermine. "I think they are finally taking hold on him!"

The *voyageur* swooped her up in his gnarled hands. "Crab
claws, my little *bonne bouche?*" he laughed. "And what
about your *beaux yeux?*"

She kissed him for the compliment, but her lips turned
serious. "I am still afraid of that beautiful one. I would not
want him to take me only because he could not have her.
Also, godfather," she added gravely, "I heard the *Huntsmen*
in the rapids just now. They were digging their paddles short
and fast to hurry away from trouble."

Hyacinthe Beauharnais crossed himself hastily. *"Dieu nous
garde,"* he muttered. "The *Huntsmen* always know when
la mauvaise fortune is near—"

2

A BARNBURNER OR THREE

At Canal Headquarters young Charles Harvey could sense
no bad luck in the offing. All during July he kept the works
humming ahead of schedule. When word came up the lakes
that Colonel Canfield, the state engineer, had died in Detroit,
the former traveling salesman sent flowers, but admitted in
private to Ringgold: "Once or twice I could have cheerfully
murdered him—especially last week when that cofferdam
of his collapsed under pressure and almost wrecked the whole
job." Harvey cocked an eye. "Remember when you said his
ghost might haunt us?"

Ringgold nodded. "Never wink at a hunch," he advised
soberly. "What worries me most right now is the way the
anti-canal crowd is playing possum."

Harvey shrugged. He had enough real troubles without
dreaming up extra difficulties. During the next week he
challenged a major engineering problem—Colonel Canfield's
useless cofferdam.

He was placed on his mettle. In addition to the anti-canal
crowd, there were important witnesses on hand to watch his

success or failure. June had seen a new political party born in Michigan at an outdoor convention under Jackson's oaks. Horace Greeley was supposed to christen the political infant, but Michigan's delegates already were calling themselves Republicans. They had nominated Kingsley S. Bingham as their candidate for governor, and then had brought him up to the Soo on a stump-tour of the state.

With Michigan's next governor on the scene to observe a traveling salesman in action, Charles T. Harvey bore in mind what Thaddeus Fairbanks once had told him and young Charles Hosmer Morse:

"Boys, all the book learning in creation can't beat hustle and common sense. I calculate you've both got hustle or I wouldn't be wasting my time with you. Common sense is just forgetting all the foolishness you've heard about everything, and studying it as if your eyes were the first to take notice, and then drawing your own conclusions. Common sense never bucks nature but always takes advantage of her laws. What I mean—March is generally a fine month for wind-mills. . . ."

So Harvey closed his ears to the discouragement of professional advice. Acting on a tip from Captain Ringgold, he bought the spare mainsails of every ship at the Soo. To the amazement of Michigan's entire corps of state engineers, their home-made experiment worked. With mainsails nailed fast to the top and held firm at the bottom with bargeloads of gravel, the cofferdam stood like a door slammed shut against Lake Superior and kept the big ditch watertight.

To celebrate, and to keep his political fences mended, Harvey invited the Republican gubernatorial candidate and the Michigan delegates to join him and a few friends at Shanty Twenty-five for a banquet of the Widow Phelan's hash, a dish now celebrated on at least two continents and requested by all famous visitors as soon as they arrived at the head of navigation.

Harvey also invited the two prettiest girls at the Soo to brighten the party, but he made his usual absent-minded botch of grouping the guests. He seated Kingsley Bingham in the place of honor next to himself, Genesee Trowbridge next to Ringgold, and Susan Marie next to Doctor Jessup.

The politicians and Harvey enjoyed the widow's hash and their own talk. The rest of the table was troubled with one-way conversations and sidelong glances. In the middle of what he considered a rather interesting explanation as to why malaria, the scourge of the Erie Canal, had not and probably would not bother the construction of the Soo Canal, Doctor Jessup stopped short.

"You haven't heard a word I've said."

"Oh, but I have," Susan Marie fibbed. "And I think a picnic is a wonderful idea."

"Picnic?" echoed Doctor Jessup. "Who said anything about a picnic?"

"Who indeed?" replied Susan Marie, and added with baffling frankness: "But a picnic has been on my mind, and it slipped out. You see, I have found a place where there are many blueberry bushes and I have been trying to tell Captain Ringgold about them because we could go on a picnic. You, too, of course!" she said in polite after-thought. "But I can't get him to listen." The Ojibway-Irish in her went on the warpath. "He is too busy making himself charming to somebody else. But she isn't listening to him either, and it serves him right!"

Ringgold had been informing Genesee about the engineering job on the cofferdam. "Aboard ship we patch up most of our worries with sailcloth," he was explaining. "If the *Huron Belle* ripped herself open on the rocks, we might be able to lower a sail alongside and cover the damage. During the Battle of Lake Erie, so the oldtimers say, cannonball holes were——" His voice bogged down, and his fork rapped her plate. "You aren't listening."

"I certainly am listening," Genesee denied, coloring a little. "But I'm afraid I missed your last remark."

"You mean my last couple of hundred," Ringgold grinned. "But I hate to play second fiddle in your ears to the tune Harvey and Bingham are playing."

"Politics," Genesee said, "I'm so sick of hearing politics!"

"Take me," Ringgold said, "I'm not against the Republicans or the Liberty Whigs or the Free-Soilers, or any of these new parties, but I'll always kind of favor the Barnburners. I don't know anything about their political platform, but I like the sound of their name." His eyes danced. "Any particular barn you'd like burned?"

"It might be *one* way of attracting his attention!"

"I know whose barn I would burn down," Susan Marie broke in, "if he *had* a barn, instead of a boat!"

3

TEETOTAL COURTSHIP

After the banquet, Genesee lingered in the moonlight outside Shanty Twenty-five, but it was Ringgold who offered his arm back to the Van Anden House, while Susan Marie kicked at stones as she strolled along with Doctor Jessup for an escort.

Harvey, with his heart in his work and no eye for a lovely girl under the moon, took Kingsley S. Bingham and the rest of the new Republicans to Elmwood as his overnight guests. By late lamplight he wrote the Fairbanks Brothers:

GENTLEMEN: With use of Colonel Canfield's coffer dam now essential, it was tested but failed to stand ultimate pressure, & collapsed. A fearful disaster in having Lake Superior pour through the unfinished canel & locks was barely averted. After 3 repair failures, state engineers agreed to let our staff attempt to solve problem. Pleased to report job accomplished today & under observance of

Michigan's next governor, if present political trend con-
tinues. The ditch is now bone-dry for work crews & am
entertaining Mr. Bingham & party at company expense
for good-will purposes.

Am glad to submit following facts & figures for company files: a depth of 12 feet at mean stage has been
achieved in the canal work; canal being paved where
cutting was not through rock; both locks well under construction near foot of canal; lift of upper lock, 8 feet;
lower lock, 10 feet; lower pier, 180 feet long, 20 feet wide;
upper pier, 830 feet long, from 16 to 30 feet wide; upper
gate, 17 feet high; lower gate, 24 feet 6 inches high; also
in receipt of upper and lower caisson gates to shut off water
from canal; estimate 103,437 lbs. of wrought iron used in
gates, & 38,000 lbs. cast iron; estimate 3,157 kegs of Delaware blasting powder; estimate 320,000 total days' labor;
facestone for locks being laid in regular courses with ir-
regular bond & have bush-hammered faces with 1½ inch
margin draft, & joints have beds cut to ⅜ inch; walls of
locks 25 feet high, ten feet thick at bottom; canal walls
smoothed and sloped ½ to 1; limestone for walls obtained
from Malden, Canada, & Marblehead, Ohio; the limestone
backing from Drummond Island near mouth of St. Mary's
River.

Captain Ringgold conveys his respects to Mr. Charles
Hosmer Morse & is in agreement that greatest city on Great
Lakes, if not whole world, will be Chicago, but Detroit's
no slouch, neither is Cleveland, & every port along the
Seaway from the height of freshwater at Superior City to
tidewater at Montreal & Quebec on the St. Lawrence will
bear watching.

The boat that took Harvey's political guests back toward
Lansing met other boats headed upstream and loaded to the
rails with new workers. The canal ate a man a day, so the
Irish said, and when newcomers landed, the veterans hollered: "Here's fresh meat for the Old Lady!"

They seldom arrived Presbyterian sober, and they were
mostly leavings of the Lakes, but Harvey hammered them into
men, or paved them into his Big Ditch.

The only relief from work tension all summer was Patrick Flynn's courtship of Michael Phelan's widow. With his place aboard the *Huron Belle* taken by his sour Scot friend Angus Laing, Pat worshipped at the shrine of Shanty Twenty-five. "It's my very life I'd give up for you," he said rashly.

First the bonny widow asked him to give up his Crabapple Cut Plug, and then he swore off his jug of Rumbellion. When she accused him of not keeping his pledges, he studied the problem and, knowing her faith in the powers of a paper, finally produced a document embellished with a great red and gold seal.

Into her kitchen he strode to wave scroll and seal under the sweet tilt of her nose. "And would you be reading this now with your own dainty eyes and still be doubting my word?" he asked in high triumph.

"And would you be reciting it to me in that grand voice of yours?" countered the widow who could not read. And she nodded a respectful greeting to every impressive flourish on the document.

> I, Patrick Flynn, do hereby solemnly swear that I will never touch the sinful weed nor the demon rum again, so help me, Temperance! . . . Signed and acknowledged before me this 29th day of July, 1854, Henry M. Dodge, Esquire, Justice of the Peace, Chippewa County, Upper Peninsula, Michigan.

"There," said Pat after he had read the document in a resounding voice, "that settles the matter. Even if you thought you saw me staggering drunk and spitting grasshopper juice from my ears, you'd know it must be your own eyes deceiving you, and not myself, because here's the real evidence in black and white for you to hold."

He made a ceremony of handing her the pledge. "There's no denying such a document. Do you think Squire Dodge would sign and seal his name to a lie? And now that I've given up everything worth living for, except my hope of heaven and your own sweet self," sighed Patrick Flynn, "how long must I be kept dangling on a string for your answer?"

Down into the widow's plump bosom went the paper. "It's attracted I am to your clodhopping ways and your face like the map of Ireland," she admitted. "But, until Mister Harvey's canal is finished, I can't be sparing the time to give a *yes* or a *no* or a *maybe* to the likes of you and your blarney-tongued tribe."

"Until the canal's finished?" groaned Pat. "That's a million years from now. And there's some who say Harvey won't ever finish the job."

"Then I'll never get married again!" vowed the widow.

But, as Patrick Flynn pulled a long face and scuffed toward the door, she cast him a sidelong glance and blushed as rosy as any bride-to-be. "Come back here, you big booby," she called. "For a woman needs more than a mirror to tell her how she looks, as anyone but a great lump would understand. And sure, until Mister Harvey's work is done and I have time to make up my mind to what I've already decided, did I say anything against a smack and a squeeze every once in awhile?"

4

VOICES IN THE RAPIDS

July was ready to be torn off the calendar, but it would have taken an axe to wipe the smile from Patrick Flynn's face as he paraded around the Soo that week, with his thumbs stuck jauntily in the armholes of his vest and his toes tapping tunes on the ground.

"You're acting as proud," said Ringgold, "as if you'd made every good Irishman's pilgrimage back to Erin and kissed the Blarney Stone."

"Kiss the Blarney Stone?" said Pat, with a secret in his eyes. "Where's the joy or comfort in kissing a cold slab of rock? I've better things to be doing with my time." And he went whistling toward Shanty Twenty-five.

Ringgold chuckled the widow's beau out of sight, but then he turned toward the river where he had seen Susan Marie sitting on a rock only a few stepping stones from shore. From a distance, in her white dress, she seemed a water lily sprung peek-a-bloom at the edge of St. Mary's Falls.

Walking in the girl's direction, Ringgold frowned. He was worried about her. Nobody would ever call Susan Marie pretty as a picture, because ordinarily she came busting out of the frame. But now she had changed into a regular sobersides, and it bothered him to see her liveliness gone.

"Hello, gloomy Gus," he said, crossing the stepping stones to sit beside her on the rock. "Let's you and me go toss bricks through windows or pour salt in sugar bowls or do something to put a smile back on your face." He yanked, not too hard, at a red hairbow. "Have I done anything to make you mad, or sad, or whatever it is?"

"Oh, no," said Susan Marie. "You haven't done anything to make me mad." Her lips curved a little. "I mean, no more than usual."

"Then why do you come mooning down here every day and go sleep-walking home as if tomorrow might be the end of the world. What's wrong?"

"I wish I knew. I have been listening to the *Voices of the Rapids.*" Her face took on more worry-wrinkles as she leaned toward the rush and foam of St. Mary's Falls. "Even now I can hear the *Voices* — as if many canoes were being paddled against the current while the *Mist People* talk to one another. I must go home and tell my godfather that his *Hunstmen* are hurrying today more than ever, dipping their paddles quick and sharp, calling:

"*Faster, faster! Trouble upstream! Faster, faster! Vole, mon coeur, vole!*"

"You shouldn't get all worked up like this," Ringgold said uncomfortably. "I don't hear anything."

"And because you don't hear anything, you think there is nothing to hear!" flashed Susan Marie. "You think it is all nonsense!" She lifted her skirts across the stepping stones and stormed at him from the bank. "Maybe someday you will hear the *Mist People,* but not before you learn to hear the voice of your own heart!" Ringgold stared after her, scowling.

5

Plague Flag

In August, Harvey increased his gangs to three thousand strong, and he bossed them with a voice that could crack a whip or blow a bugle. Six days a week, bragged the Irish, he slave-drove them on the job, and on Sunday he drove them to church.

Late one afternoon a seasoned gang was setting dead-men ties to bolster the canal locks when Mike Shanahan doubled up with cramps. The rest of them, recalling last summer's false alarm, saw nothing ominous in the scene, and Mike's bunkmates joked about rotgut whisky as they carted him off for treatment.

A few minutes after sundown the Irishman was dead.

Doctor Jessup called Harvey to the company hospital on Rapids Island. "No false alarm this time," he said heavily. "It's Asiatic cholera."

Harvey passed the word to the pair that could be trusted in any crisis. "We're the burial squad," he told Ringgold and Patrick Flynn, and by dark of moon they dug a grave in the woods to hide Shanahan's body.

Late into the night Harvey laid down the law to his lieutenants. "But you can't expect to keep the plague a secret," objected Foreman Chapel.

"Not for long, but I expect to keep the gangs guessing. I'll stop at nothing to maintain a full working force."

Next morning they saw another side of his character as he chartered the propellor *Napoleon* for an impromptu excursion on Lake Superior. All wives, children, and sweethearts of canal workers were invited to take the cruise. There were only two holdouts. Michael Phelan's widow refused to budge, although she permitted her three daughters to go in Susan Marie's care. Genesee Trowbridge held herself apart, a vision in cool green, her parasol a shield against the crowd. "For the last time, no!" she told Ringgold. "I don't want to go for a boat ride with that—*swarm.*"

The young lakeman played his trump card, a lie. "Suit yourself, but Harvey said he'd like you to go along and sort of keep things on an even keel."

"Oh?" breathed Genesee. "Well, of course, in that case—"

It was a gala occasion above the rapids as the *Napoleon* blew for clearing and handkerchiefs from docks and deck fluttered gay good-bys. Only the *Huntsmen,* the *Mist People,* knew that many of the farewells were forever, because one tenth of Harvey's force was doomed to die of cholera.

Puzzled by lack of instruction, Captain Clark—once he had the *Napoleon* ready to slip her moorings—approached Harvey and asked: "How long you want this cruise to last?"

Harvey glanced around quickly, replied in a low voice. "Until the plague flag comes down from Point Iroquois."

"Plague flag?" he echoed blankly. "There's none flying."

Harvey's eyes were grim. "There will be!"

Three more canallers died that week, and the burial squad managed to hush the deaths, but when five people died in town the lid blew off. Half the Soo's regular inhabitant's booked passage to Marquette or Copper Harbor. Overnight, shops were shuttered up; the bars tripled their business.

The anti-canal faction reacted in typical style. Fat Philo Worts skipped west on the first boat. Doctor Musgrave tried to hide in a bottle, Cole Slater hoped for his employer's death so he could get control of the portage company's accounts. Daniel Trowbridge ordered smudge-heaps of Youghiogheny coal spaced along Water Street to fight the sickness in the air, and Jay Bisby's next editorial in the *Soo Sentinel* blamed the cholera epidemic on Harvey and his canal.

The day the paper splashed its scarehead news, almost a hundred men deserted the diggings. Fear stalked the camp, the smell of it so strong that dogs growled and snapped at their masters.

Oldtimers brought nightmares out of their memories to tell the others what had been the result of past attacks. "Worst I ever seen was in Detroit in '32," said a grizzled blacksmith. "That's when the cholera came up the lakes on the *Henry Clay*. She was carrying soldiers for the Black Hawk War, but most of them never lived to fight. I seen thirty buried in a common grave at Ste. Anne's Church, and I'll declare to my dying day that at least one of them was still alive. I seen his hand move!"

A pitman nodded solemnly. "I believe you," he said. "Lookit what happened in Cincinnati only five years ago," he told the rest of the canallers. "One month we had us a housing shortage, but the next month — three thousand vacant homes! Fourth of July week we buried eleven hundred, with drunk drivers racing their hearses to the cemeteries and spilling out coffins at every bump and turn in the road. Nobody cared. It was either get religion or get as much fun as fast as you could before the cholera got you!"

After supper the gangs, more full of grim stories than food, milled around the unfinished locks, and only one spark was needed to stampede them toward Minnesota Territory.

Into that shaky world pranced a mouse-colored mare with a mad gleam in her eye and a nip of her yellowed teeth for any slowpoke in her way. With Harvey at the reins she was drawing—wonder of wonders—a wagonload of whisky barrels, and Michael Phelan's widow sat atop one of them wearing a smile like the red rose of Sharon.

Flanked by Captain Ringgold and Patrick Flynn, Harvey faced his toughest customers, with a plague to sell. "There's cholera in camp, boys, but no need for alarm. Our cases have been light, and Doctor Jessup has the situation under control. The town's been hard hit, but what can you expect from run-down constitutions and a worthless doctor? The canal company's got the only hospital north of Detroit, trained nurses, the finest—"

"Foosh to all that blarney!" roared a burly Mick. "Sure, and there's no cure for cholera!"

Up popped the widow on her barrel. "Nor for cowards!" she cried. "Stop by the shanty on your hike to the tall timber and I'll borrow you some petticoats, because you don't belong in pants!" She poked at her war bonnet and glared at the shamefaced wretch. "The beat of my heart and second helpings of hash for them that stays, but bad cess and the back of my hand to all quitters!" Her voice rang with scorn. "Faith, and I'm just back from a visit to Mike Shanahan, and you should have seen him, a slice of cake in his mouth and a pretty nurse to each elbow in case he wants more."

The bonny widow's story, for which she was already mumbling a hundred *Hail Marys* in penance, galvanized the canal gangs. Think of it now, Mike Shanahan still alive, and him taken sick a whole week ago, not overly strong to begin with, not delicate, mind you, but never a lad to straighten out horseshoes with his bare fists neither, and if suchlike as him could be cured of the cholera and live to eat cake and hold hands with colleens, by the beard of St. Brendan go bring on your plague!

Harvey, the teetotal abstainer, seized the psychological moment to explain the whisky barrels. "As a precautionary measure Doctor Jessup recommends four drams of strong spirits daily. Although I'm still opposed to all intoxicants, they will

be regarded for the duration as medical supplies and issued
therefore to all workers at canal-company expense—"

Thunderstruck, the gangs stared. Patrick Flynn banged a
tin dipper on an opened barrel. "Step up and take your medicine like men!" he bellowed, to make the situation clear.
As they came elbowing forward, he sampled the Monongahela
and heaved a gusty sigh for the widow's benefit. "Ah, Mrs.
Phelan, it's not breaking my temperance pledge to you, but
following orders I am," he said, smacking his lips. "Sure, and
you've got to admit this is just what the doctor ordered!"

Laughter boomed out and fear scuttled away, but that was
only the first skirmish. Harvey and Ringgold realized that the
cholera war would last until the crackling frost of October
routed the enemy. Meanwhile, Sault Ste. Marie turned into a ghost town. Soot from the smudge-heaps fell thick as
black snow along Water Street and Portage Avenue. But
Daniel Trowbridge found that not even sulphur thrown on
the fires could drive away the death that went everywhere . . .

6

THE BURIAL SQUAD

On the canal the toll soared from three a week in August
to three a day in September, but Harvey lashed his gangs
without letup, keeping them working by keeping them guessing, driving them so long and so hard that they had small time
and less energy to figure out the truth. He staggered shifts,
mixed up crews, switched men from shanty to shanty, to prevent them from discovering how their original ranks had
thinned. The straw bosses had glib answers to quiet all sus-
picions:

"Where's Mike Shanahan? Sent to Mackinac Island at company expense to get back his full health. What about the Ca-
rey twins? Why, they asked for a transfer to the Drummond
quarry. Freedman? He's at the lumber camp on Garden

River. Now, tuck in your tongues and get back on the job, or no whisky-ration come whistle-blow!"

Every morning, quick as the gangs piled out of the shanties and into the cut, Captain Ringgold and Patrick Flynn made their rounds, collecting the dead and the dying from their bunks. Every midnight the mouse-colored mare plodded from the hospital deep into the woods where—while Flynn fingered his rosary and Ringgold leaned on his shovel—Harvey spoke the funeral rites.

On the second Friday in October a cold wave howled down from Hudson Bay, but there were nineteen bodies to be stacked like cord-wood in the plague wagon. The burial squad, bone-weary and heartsick, had its largest common grave to dig. Then, as Ringgold held aloft a pine torch, Patrick Flynn read the list of victims and Harvey told them good-by:

"Ryan, Miller, McBride, Saxton, Kelly! *The Lord is my shepherd, I shall not want.* Flaherty, O'Reilly, Cash, Magruder, Malone! *He leadeth me beside the still waters.* Woodbridge, McTavish, Smith, Calloway, Neilsen! *Yea, though I walk through the valley of the shadow of death, I will fear no evil.* Cohen, McCallister, Tracy, O'Brien! *And I will dwell in the house of the Lord for ever . . ."*

The three stood silent with bared heads while a bitter wind shook the hemlocks. "Ah, it doesn't seem right," sighed Patrick Flynn, gripping his shovel. "Nineteen of the salt of the earth, and not even a marker to remember the bully boys by—"

Charles Harvey wheeled toward the pine torch, the bright promise in his eyes eclipsing the worry and weariness that pinched his face. "No marker?" he cried. "They've left a monument greater than all the pyramids piled together. Their marker is the Soo Canal!"

The cold wave killed the cholera. A week later the plague flag was hauled down and Captain Clark brought home the

Napoleon. Sad news met more than a few women and children, but they had Harvey's excursion to thank for their lives, and the Soo had a sweet tooth for widows.

7

TWO LETTERS MENTION MR. WHITTIER

In Cambridge, Massachusetts, a Harvard professor who had never seen Lake Superior received another heckling letter from Sault Ste. Marie.

> DEAR COZ: Two and a half years ago I requested a simple little poem boosting Lake Superior. Since then a friend of mine has promoted a canal and is now on the last lap of connecting Lake Superior's shipping with the lower lakes. Is a poem harder to build than the Soo Canal? Come now, Cousin! Also — I hate to keep bringing up a sore point, but — Send you a wagonload of histories by Schoolcraft, and what happens? Not one rhyme in thirty months! Send J. G. Whittier a paltry eagle feather from the Soo and out roll a barrel of verses: 'He's whistling round St. Mary's Falls upon his loaded train; he's leaving on the Pictured Rocks his fresh tobacco stain.' That's a sample of Whittier for you, Coz! He flows. . . .

The Harvard professor waggled his bushy brows through the rest of the letter, which contained more of the same brand of impertinence. He burrowed among loose manuscript and the litter of Mr. Schoolcraft's books on his desk to find clean paper and a sharp quill. Then, eyes twinkling and beard chuckling, he wrote:

> MY DEAR IMPETUOUS COUSIN RINGGOLD: I am not racing a poem against a ship canal! As to the relative difficulties in building the two products, there are times when I should be glad to change places with your Mr. Harvey. However, I expect to send you a poem before the first ship passes through the Soo Canal into Lake Superior. If you are

not satisfied with the service, I can only suggest that you
change your middle name to Whittier. Until then, I must
humbly remain, your unflowing kinsman,

HENRY WADSWORTH LONGFELLOW

8

SURPRISE PARTY

This letter reached the Soo on the last boat of the season.
The steamer *Illinois* also brought Senator Cass—one of Michigan's storied figures—to inspect the canal works, and an Osgood dredge that Harvey had ordered to remove the sandbar
indicated at the pier entrance to Lake Superior on Colonel
Canfield's chart.

Sight of the dredge seemed to be a signal that Daniel Trowbridge had been awaiting. For a while he stood in the door-
way of the Portage Company office, a dead cigar between his
teeth, and watched Cole Slater boss the stevedores as they
transferred barrels of supplies for the mining camps from the
Illinois to his own horse-cars. Then he watched the cars haul
the profitable freight on rails around the rapids to where Lake
Superior ships were docked above St. Mary's Falls to take it
aboard. Finally his eyes swerved from the portage railroad
to the unfinished canal, but, before any change of expression
showed on his face, he disappeared into the office.

A few minutes later Daniel Trowbridge came out to an-
nounce a Victory Ball. He smiled blandly at those who complimented him on this sportsmanlike way of anticipating
the success of the canal company.

"Senator Cass is guest of honor, and simply everyone is
invited!" Genesee told Ringgold before Sunday service, her
voice pinking the ears of a jump-jack girl yanking at the
handrope of the church bell. "Social distinctions are so confused on the frontier that Father and I wouldn't know where
to draw the line——"

"Bless her backwards!" gritted Susan Marie. "Miss Snippy Nose!"

The Victory Ball wound up as a Surprise Party, but it began smoothly enough. Fiddles scraped in the Van Anden House, quadrilles and cotillions formed. Daniel Trowbridge poured Wellington Punch for most of his guests, raspberry shrub for the ladies and Harvey. Cole Slater and Ringgold tried to claim a dance with Genesee but, between General Cass and the officers from Fort Brady, there was no getting near her. Harvey managed, however, and just in time for the new Garland Waltz. Then a dream came true and Genesee floated away on a pink cloud.

"Sure, and you dance so light and easy," said Patrick Flynn to Michael Phelan's widow, "you could be writing songs with your toes!"

"Get along with your blarney," the widow told him, "but, faith, and you're not so clumsy yourself. I won't be saying we make the finest couple on the floor, because there's Mister Harvey swinging Miss Trowbridge around in grand style—"

"All right," said Pat. "You won't be saying we make the finest looking couple on the floor." He dipped and whirled his bonny partner for dear life. "But, *ma-vournin*, you'd better not be saying we don't!"

As the ball neared its unexpected climax, an ancient *voyageur*, scarlet-sashed and heron-plumed, appeared escorting a girl with red hairbows anchored to her Indian braids. She was wrapped to the chin in a fur cape of such barbaric extravagance that even Factor Hargreaves of the Hudson's Bay Post sucked in an awed breath. Out from that king's ransom she stepped to make a grand entrance in the ceremonial splendor of an Ojibway princess, fringed with buckskin, with the sacred bear-claw ornaments jingling from her wrist and ankles.

Proud as white pine, Susan Marie surveyed the ballroom. Her rainbow-struck-by-lightning eyes flashed at Genesee. Social distinctions?   Oho!

Senator Cass broke the spell that held the room enthralled. Leaving Genesee with her cheeks aflame, and followed by the officers, he paid his respects to Susan Marie. "Why, this young lady's great-grandmother saved my whole force from massacre not a stone's throw from here," he announced. "Otherwise, there'd be no Fort Brady today," he chuckled reminiscently. "I mind I had Henry Schoolcraft along with me that trip as a minerologist, and blamed if he didn't go fall in love with your great-aunt!" he said to Susan Marie. "Bless me, child, that's thirty-five years ago and ancient history to you, but it seems only yesterday that he carried his bride across the brand-new threshhold of Elmwood, and settled down to collect all the Algonquin legends and customs he could put his pen on.

"Only yesterday, it seems," the old gentleman repeated, "and now Mr. Harvey is staying in the same house, making history instead of writing it——"

Seething with outraged vanity, Genesee watched Harvey join the attentive circle around Susan Marie. Her slippers made angry sounds across the floor. "I opposed this whole idea of yours," she told her father in a tight voice, "because I saw no need of humiliating Mr. Harvey in public, but now——"

Daniel Trowbridge, standing with Cole Slater, studied her shrewdly. "Now what, my dear?"

"Now," Genesee blazed, "I want to make the announcement myself!"

She whirled to the bandstand, stealing the stage from Susan Marie, and commanding the room's attention with her first words:

"I want to explain this Victory Ball," she said briskly, her eyes bright as diamonds but her temper tightly leashed. "As

most of you know, my father and I have opposed the Soo
Canal from the start.   Because we were convinced it would
not only ruin the two portage companies that now carry all
the freight between the Lower Lakes and Lake Superior, but
also put an end to the year-round employment of hauling
ships around the rapids on greased ways and rollers and
sledges.   Because it would destroy the hotel and tavern and
eating house trade.   Because it would mean nothing but loss
of business and wages to Sault Ste. Marie.   There would be no
reason to stop here.   The ships would glide through the canal
and pass us by."

For a bare moment, Genesee's glance rested on Harvey.

"It's not a good feeling—to be passed by," she said slowly.
Then her voice resumed its briskness.   "But we fought and
lost, and now we concede the completion of the Soo Canal."

Her hand pushed down the premature applause.

"But there's generally a way to salvage victory from defeat.
Take this case: Mr. Harvey must finish his job by May 19th
or else the canal company dosen't get paid the seven hundred
and fifty thousand acres of timber and mineral lands, and the
State of Michigan can throw the whole grant open to public
sale.   If for any reason, Mr. Harvey should be unable to meet
that May deadline, his company would go bankrupt, Michigan would receive a free canal, and land speculators would
make fortunes.   Right, Senator Cass?"

"You have stated the situation correctly, ma'am," said An-
drew Jackson's onetime Secretary of War.

Ringgold glanced from Harvey's puzzled frown to Slater's
wolfish grin.   Land speculators.   If anything went wrong, the
Trowbridge group had the inside track.   Publisher Bisby had
charge of the U.S. Land Office in the *Sentinel* Block!

Then Genesee set off her bomb.   "My father and his associates already have formed the Wolverine Land Company.
For several months they have had private information—
kept secret even from me—that the late Colonel Canfield

marked a sandbar on the state chart where a rock ledge should
be shown! Nothing can stop the completion of the Soo Canal,
but that error will prevent its completion on schedule!" She
shot a triumphant look at the white-faced Connecticut Yankee, and held out a hand to her father. "Make no mistake
about it, Mr. Harvey, this is *our* Victory Ball!"

For a shocked moment the Van Anden House seemed
caught in the dead silence that follows a thunderclap, then
the ballroom fired into an exploding pinwheel of faces whirl-
ing around a tightlipped Harvey and the jealous girl who
had pronounced his doom. Captain Ringgold had his hands
full trying to keep a wild Irish Indian out of trouble.

"Let me go!" she blazed in fierce loyalty. "If I were Mr.
Harvey, I would tear her heart out and——"

His hand clamped over her mouth and he tried to yell some
sense into her temper-tossed eyes. "Pipe down on those
threats, Little Sister!"

Susan Marie wrenched free. Little Sister! That was the
last straw. Her palm stung itself against his cheek. "Go
ahead and defend her. See if I care! Me, I know when I'm not
wanted!"

Before Ringgold could stop her, she slipped through the
crowd, calling for Hyacinthe Beauharnais. In the press and
confusion of bodies she never felt Cole Slater pounce at her
wrist to snatch a broken bear-claw bracelet.

9

MURDER AND FLIGHT

In less than an hour the Baptist Mission Bell rang frantic
alarm through the night. After the Victory Ball's sudden
breakup, Daniel Trowbridge had gone for his usual stroll before bed. Minutes later an Irish canaller, tipsy as a wheelbarrow, stumbled across Trowbridge's body in an alleyway
and yelled bloody murder when he saw the knife sticking out

between the shoulder blades. Investigation disclosed a broken bear-claw bracelet nearby, and suspicion hardened into virtual certainty when a half-breed reported seeing Hyacinthe Beauharnais and his goddaughter paddling furiously down the St. Mary's in a pack-heavy Nor'west canoe.

"Skipped bag and baggage, and if that doesn't prove them guilty of murder, what more do you want?" growled Slater, but he scoffed at a search party. "Easier to track an eagle through the air than those two!"

During the black watch before grey dawn Ringgold dropped in at Shanty Twenty-five for breakfast, and to bluster about Susan Marie's innocence to Patrick Flynn and Michael Phelan's widow. "But there's a wild streak in her," he said uneasily, "and—why did she leave town?"

"There's two reasons a woman runs away; to make a man chase after her or to let him cool his heels and find out how much he's missing by not having her around!" She gave Patrick Flynn a smile sweeter than the maple sirup he was pouring on her flapjacks. "And let that be a lesson to both of you big boobies!"

"Ah, what do you know about women?" said Pat fondly. "Sure, and you're only a woman yourself—may the Saints be praised for it!"

That morning Harvey and his canal lieutenants, hauling the Osgood dredge to the pier entrance of Lake Superior, fought ice and bone-chilling seas to work instruments to learn that Genesee Trowbridge had told the truth. Instead of the sandbar that could have been removed easily, a rock ledge lurked under the gray waves, a reef that would rip the bottom out of any ship entering the canal, a reef that now wrecked all of Harvey's hopes.

Had Trowbridge bribed Canfield, or had the state engineer blundered? It made no practical difference. True to Ringgold's hunch, the Colonel's ghost had come back to haunt Harvey.

When Harvey and Ringgold made a dispirited return to Canal Headquarters, they found Genesee waiting for them. She wore deep mourning and her features were tear-stained. There was on awkward moment while the men clumsily offered their condolences.

"If there's anything we can do——" Ringgold spoke for both of them.

Her fingers twisted a handkerchief. "I came to apologize——"

"No need." Harvey, the realist, stopped her. "Your announcement about a rock ledge came as a shock, but it worked no real harm. *It's the fact that a rock ledge exists that does the damage.* Neither you nor your father nor Cole Slater put it there."

Curiosity flicked in Ringgold's glance at Genesee. "Why didn't they let you in on the secret sooner?"

She had been looking straight at Harvey; now she dropped her eyes and flushed slightly. "Can any woman be trusted with a secret?"

"Depends," said Ringgold. "I'm betting you would have tipped us off and given us a fighting chance."

"No!" Genesee exclaimed too quickly. "My father—" the tears sounded in her voice—"fought the canal because he was honestly convinced that it would not only ruin his business but turn Sault Ste. Marie into a ghost town. He came up here a sick man and he had to use Cole Slater as his fist. Last night was his hour of triumph, but it lasted such a little while— and now it's all so useless!"

Harvey's heavy nod showed complete understanding.

Ringgold's quick sympathy reached both of them, but he spoke to the girl. "Any plans?"

Genesee regained her composure. "I'm going to try to sell the portage company. I've already given Slater his walking papers. By partnership agreement he gets my father's Wolverine Land shares. I'm glad of that," she added. "With Father gone, I won't tolerate Slater or his crowd."

"Those shares may prove a gold mine now," Harvey said.

Ringgold stared at the other two. They made a good pair. He hoped to bring them together someday. Trowbridge's death had raised one mystery, but it had solved an emotional problem for Ringgold. He realized, now that Susan Marie had fled, that he was head over heart in love with her and, like all lovers, he wanted to play marriage broker. Again he spoke in her defense.

"Those land shares could be the motive," he said. "I'd stake my life that Susan Marie and Beauharnais are innocent, but Slater stood to profit by your father's murder."

"What's the difference who killed him?" Genesee rose to go, her eyes forlorn. "He's dead. Finding his murderer won't bring him back to life."

Harvey's troubled glance followed her out the door. "Find out what time the services are being held," he told Ringgold curtly. "Somebody's got to stand by her."

Directly after the funeral, Harvey summoned his staff to Canal Headquarters. Slumped behind the desk, he listened to Lee Nichols give a veteran engineer's opinion of their predicament: "We'd have to build another cofferdam to hold back the water while we blasted out the rock ledge. We need at least a six-month extension of time beyond May 19th. And, boys, I'm talking sense!"

Ringgold hurled the only challenge, the one denial of defeat. "Who's asking you to talk sense? If everybody talked sense and listened to reason, this country wouldn't even be discovered yet!"

But the spark failed to leap the gap to Harvey. In his report to the directors of the St. Mary's Falls Ship Canal Company, the bones of his character stood out gaunt and true. He offered no alibis. He stated only that a sandbar on the gov-

ernment chart had proved on investigation to be a rock reef.
Then he set down the blunt details:

> This reef or ledge of solid rock tapers from 1 inch to
> 3 feet in thickness & covers an area of 100 feet wide by 300
> feet long, or over 30,000 square yards. I herewith enclose
> opinion & advice of Mr. Nichols. Because of the power-
> ful lobby of land speculators in Lansing, I see no chance
> of a time extension. I most anxiously await your instruc-
> tions in this matter. . . .

The final words showed how low in mind he had sunk.
He was no longer the bull-through-trouble, gangway-for-to-
morrow Harvey, but an ordinary man waiting to be told what
to do.

10

TROUBLE IS THE SPUR

The bad news travelled fast. In his office in Michigan's
statehouse, the Honorable William Austin Burt of solar compass fame shot off a messenger to the Soo. "Tell Harvey he's
right as rain about a time extension. He hasn't got a China-
man's chance in Hangtown of getting one. Why, Lansing
wasn't even a fly speck on the map until a land lobby climbed
aboard a gravy train and moved the state capital from Dee-
troit to here. That's how strong the speculators are in this
neck of the woods. They're putting on so much political pressure, you can almost hear the money change hands. Tell
Harvey he's got to meet his deadline, or they'll have easy
pickings on a gone goose!"

There were plenty of slippery customers in Lansing, but
almost as many honest gentlemen who gave the few supporters of an extension a stout answer that was hard to contra-
dict: "If we allow leeway in this case, we establish a danger-
ous precedent. Future companies of this kind could always
find an excuse for not completing public improvements on

time. No, sir. A contract's a contract, a bargain's a bargain. The State can't afford to make exceptions."

Michigan's incoming governor, swept into office by the fledgling Republican party, remembered the traveling salesman he had watched in action at the Soo. In his inaugural address, Kingsley S. Bingham expressed his faith in the canal builder but his very compliments shrewdly avoided the necessity of making any promises:

> "This great national highway, this noble work of internal improvement, rivaling in its magnitude and in fitness and excellence of its structure the most celebrated works of a similar character in the Old World, has been prosecuted with an energy highly creditable to the able direction under which it has been constructed. A less diligent and energetic management would have been intimidated by the serious obstacles which have been interposed to impede the progress of the work. As it is, it will undoubtedly be completed within the time specified by the contract for its construction —"

The realities of the situation, and the *Soo Sentinel* editorials widely copied in the press, more than overbalanced Governor Bingham's vote of confidence. After a brief rally, Canal Company stock hit the skids as uneasy shareholders got out from under.

As soon as Harvey's report reached the East, a number of emergency meetings were called in New York. Grave-faced men from Albany, Boston, Syracuse, Detroit, and St. Johnsbury converged on the corner of William and Wall Street. They consulted McAlpine and Clark, two of the nation's best engineers. McAlpine had advised the Austrian government on the improvement of the Danube River sea entrance, and he delivered his verdict:

"Sorry, gentlemen, but we agree with the findings of Mr. Nichols. A new cofferdam is the only answer."

The directors chafed at delay. Their hands were tied until Spring unlocked the lakes. Then, they decided, they would take the first boat to the Soo. It was their intention to complete the canal in hopes that Michigan would allow an extension of time at the last minute or, failing in that, to fight for the land through court action.

"Our chances are thin," President Corning of the New York Central told Brooks of the Michigan Central.

While his two brothers spoke for the family, Thaddeus Fairbanks stared out of the window. Not much of a view—stone walls and steel cages. Now, you take trouble. Trouble was the spur that got a man going, if he had the right stuff in him. Look at that hemp business he'd started back in Vermont. Just about lost his shirt, but then he'd got to figuring out a better method of weighing up all those wagonloads of hemp he couldn't sell, and pretty soon he had a going concern—Fairbanks Scales. For a fact, the scales were younger than young Harvey, and already better known clear around the world than any other American product. Yep, when the right kind of man got into trouble, he invented himself out of it. Now, you take Charles Harvey. Why, just a couple years ago, the bumptious sport had been peddling scales, and here he was, selling a canal—maybe! Anyway, this would be the test. Trouble was the spur.

Thaddeus Fairbanks came out of his daydream to beckon his other favorite Charles—Charles Hosmer Morse. "No use pulling at your chin to try and look older in front of me, son," he chuckled. "I don't see the shadow of a beard, and I know you weren't born until Fairbanks and Company's third birthday, which makes you about old enough to vote, but not many minutes older."

The middle-aged inventor winked. "Still practicing how Fairbanks, *Morse* and Company would look on our business correspondence? Well, here's another executive decision to make. What would you do in Harvey's shoes?"

Young Mr. Morse stroked his beardless chin, but the steady resolve in his wide-set eyes and the strong lines of his mouth asked no favors nor made any apologies for his youth. "I would finish what I started, and finish it on time," he said, pushing his voice deep to make it sound older. "I don't know how I'd do it," he added honestly, his voice jumping, "but I'd do it!"

Thaddeus Fairbanks nodded. "That's the secret, son. *Will* power beats *won't* power every time. We'll have to wait and see which way Harvey tips the scales."

11

WINDOW SHOPPING IN MONTREAL

Even before Harvey's letter to the canal company directors reached the East, the wilderness telegraph system of talking drums and medicine mirrors and smoke signals had reported Susan Marie's arrival in Montreal where her godfather had left her with the Beaufait branch of her family while the hardy old *voyageur,* racing the great white cold in a navigator's straight line west along the forty-sixth parallel——historic paddle-and-portage route of Champlain, Marquette, and La Salle—followed the Ottawa River over Lake Nipissing to Georgian Bay, and so returned to Drummond Island where he hibernated with a keg of brandy and a *Mist-People* premonition that he would be needed at the Soo before the keg ran dry.

In the gay whirl of Montreal, every young gallant in town courted Susan Marie and she wore out a pair of dancing slippers a week. One of her admirers was an English nobleman who prided his artistic ability higher than his title. Lord Dunbar invited her to his studio overlooking the St. Lawrence and, with several Beaufait cousins for chaperones, she climbed castle steps to the watch tower that had been converted into his workroom.

Of special interest was a charcoal sketch of the Great Lakes, and models in clay that carried out the theme of the

sketch. "You see what I have in mind," Lord Dunbar said.
"It is a group statue that would also serve as a beautiful
fountain for perhaps a park or square."

"A charming fancy, *M'sieu*," said Susan Marie, "to imagine
each of our lakes as a tall and lovely water nymph."

"Naiads," Lord Dunbar amplified. "Cupbearers to the
gods. Whatever one chooses to call them. In the statue
group they must stand on different levels and hold above their
heads containers of various shapes to illustrate how nature has
placed and proportioned them in her scheme. For instance,
as the fountain plays, the surplus waters will *pour* from the
high brimming *basins* of Superior, Michigan, and Huron to
flow across the shallow *plate* of Erie and *plunge* or *fall* into
the deep *bowl* of Ontario."

Susan Marie's compliments made the Englishman flush
with pleasure, but then she turned to a window and gazed
out pensively on the St. Lawrence as it rolled the overflow
of all the inland seas toward the Atlantic.

"I know someone who sees the lakes in another way," she
said in a low voice. "To him they are five pretty sisters dressed
up in blue gowns and white bonnets. He thinks of them as
his sweetwater sweethearts. He speaks of the rivers that
unite them as the ribbons they wear. Do you know what he
calls the mighty St. Lawrence, *M'sieu?* Ontario ribbon! Is it
not droll?"

Judging from his expression, Lord Dunbar saw nothing
droll in the matter. "This person," he said, hesitating.
"This someone. I take it, he means a great deal to you."

"He means less than nothing!" flared Susan Marie. "Me,
I don't even despise him enough to hate him!"

But much of a certain young lady's leisure in Montreal was
spent window-shopping with a pert nose pressed white against
the pane. *Would he like her in this better than that, or would
the crocus-yellow catch his fancy? Not that she cared a snap*

*of her thumb for what he thought, but —— that flower print
might catch his eye!*

12

HARVARD PROFESSOR

In Cambridge that fateful January of 1855, Professor
Longfellow consulted his chaste Boston newspaper. Cousin
Ringgold had been so enthusiastic about that canal, and here
the shares had taken another drop. What they needed up
there was the legendary strong man named Kwasind, described in Mr. Schoolcraft's works, the one who had helped
Manabozho clear the rivers and streams, this strongest of all
men, Kwasind, who had scooped up sandbars and huge rocks
with his hands, kicked sunken logs out of the water, and made
a pathway for the people. Hmmmmmm! That line had a
good ring. *Made a pathway for the people.* Excellent! He
had a notion to fit the legend right into the poem he had
promised Cousin Ringgold by spring. Too bad the canal had
no Kwasind to call upon in this crisis, but—really it would
be sinful to waste such a well-turned line!

A New England poet could make the Lake Superior strong
man, Kwasind, come to life with ink and imagination, but
none of Kwasind's spirit showed now in Charles Harvey. At
Sault Ste. Marie, where the magic name of Manabozho on the
lips of Susan Marie's great-grandmother had helped prevent
a savage uprising against the canal, a traveling salesman had
come to full stop.

Day after day Harvey stared bleakly out the frosted windows of Canal Headquarters. He saw gangs of canallers who
could buck blizzards and forty-below weather to carry out almost any order, and he blamed himself for having no orders
to give.

Those were slim days on the diggings, and the Potato Famine Irish marked the change in Harvey. Sure, and the Old Man was not himself this winter, but off his feed on a diet of humble pie, singing small and moping around like a common desk engineer instead of sighting his level by the wheeling beams of the Northern Lights and striding down the right of way with the shadow of him taller than a white pine and his tracks in the snow the size of seven-league boots. Faith, and it fair made you weep to see how the starch had gone from him.

Harvey's spirits hit bottom the first of February when a letter from the directors came up the Snowshoe Pike by Ojibway mailman. His face lengthening, Harvey read it and pushed it across the desk to Ringgold. "They're easing me out. Hiring McAlpine and Clark to build a cofferdam."

Ringgold had one more sermon churning inside him to roar Harvey from the doldrums. "So you're going to take orders from strangers and admit you're whipped? You're going to sit slackjawed and wait for another guy to do the job? That's not how this country was built, brother. That attitude never blazed a trail anywhere!"

Slumped behind his desk, Harvey muttered. "Tell me how to beat a rock ledge."

"You've got to tell yourself, brother, and you've got to hear it in your heart! If a man really wanted, he could rip out a rock ledge with his bare hands, grind it in his teeth for gravel, and pave the future with it!"

Ringgold leaned across the desk and shook a large fist in Harvey's face. "A man's got to be as good an anvil as he is a hammer, he's got to be able to take blows as well as give them, but there comes a time during trouble when he has to stop being an anvil and start being a hammer again!"

For a split second Harvey sat as if a thunderbolt had struck him. Then he leaped up, new worlds in his eyes. "That's the answer!" he roared. "A hammer!"

13

HARVEY'S HAMMER

Even Ringgold gulped when he heard the idea his words had planted full-bloom in Harvey's head. Lee Nichols had a conniption fit. "You can't build any such contraption," the old Erie Canal engineer declared. "The Soo's locked up and winter's thrown away the key! We're four hundred miles from the nearest machine shop, and that's by snowshoe trail! Try another brainstorm, son. No use wasting time on something you can't make in the first place and that won't work in the second place!"

His jaw set, Harvey faced his lieutenants. "Now that we know what we're up against, let's get going!"

When the word got around, the Irish dubbed the new project, *Harvey's Hammer*. He called it a steam punch. It took shape slowly across the swift weeks as relays of blacksmiths toiled at the forge while a battery of seven mighty bellows blew at the fire to blast the iron white-hot for the engine the boss had ordered.

A Detroit machine shop would have had trouble making the three-ton punch Harvey wanted to smash the rock ledge. The little blacksmith shop beside the canal locks almost went up in smoke and sparks trying to meet his demands. Six days a week it aped Dante's Inferno, but on the seventh day the bellows rested.

"Throwing away a day a week," warned Ringgold, "might cost you a canal!"

"When a man gives up his principles to gain something, he makes a bad bargain," Harvey said stubbornly.

As March blew in with a sub-zero roar, the two young swashbucklers tramped the lumberjack skidways and cruised the woods to locate a white oak five feet thick at the snow line. Their eyes glistened at sight of the giant towering more than a hundred feet toward the stars.

"Handle her gently, boys!" hollered Ringgold. "Because she sprang from an acorn before Columbus sailed in search of the Indies, and she was born to make history on the Soo Canal—"

"Tim-ber!" They snaked the tough old lady over a trail that had been watered down to provide an icy bed for her bones.

"I want a stick thirty feet long and fourteen inches square," Harvey told his carpenters. "Carve it out of her stout heart to make a shaft for my steam punch."

He had a bugle to his lips again and he was blowing for gangway into Lake Superior. The Wolverine Land Company, controlled by Doctor Musgrave, Slater, Bisby and Worts, began to sit up and take worried notice. Cole Slater stroked the black stubble of his whiskers. No question about Harvey's being a madman, but—suppose his madness worked?

In the *Soo Sentinel*, Jay Bisby took blustering notice of Harvey's unhinged mind. From Genesee Trowbridge, he crowed, Harvey had bought every available tramcar only to rip off the axles and throw the rest in the dump. But his crowning folly, hooted the publisher, was his purchase of a lake steamer that he chopped from the ice and hauled out of the water merely to remove a couple of wrought-iron propeller blades.

"Bisby must be getting nervous," Harvey chuckled to Ringgold. "We'll bolt those axles to the sides of the steam punch for extra gravity, and we'll make those blades into a socket for holding the oak shaft to the metal hammer head."

In such fashion the steam punch grew, and truly, trouble was the spur. The second Saturday in March saw *Harvey's*

Hammer almost complete. His canal lieutenants secretly plotted a Sunday shift to finish the job, and Michael Phelan's widow whisked her three small daughters to Elmwood for an all-day visit to keep the boss occupied.

"Sure, and what his holiness don't know won't be hurting him," said Patrick Flynn, as he helped work the battery of forge bellows for the blacksmiths between swigs from his jug of Rumbellion. "Which saying," he winked, "could be applied to my own dainty darling, and, faith, if an Irishman was meant to be perfect, then why was I made the exception to prove the rule, and will you be answering me that in your absence, Mrs. Phelan, will you now, for it's niver an argument I've won with you yet, when your own sweet self is around—"

14

JUNGLE LAW UNDER THE NORTH STAR

With a broken Sabbath and a rousing day's work behind them, the crew closed shop and plowed home through the night. But Patrick Flynn reached his own shanty only to turn around and start back, mulishly resisting Ringgold's arguments.

"And do you think I've a heart of paving brick to leave my poor jug of Rumbellion all alone in the dark through the whole bristling night, worrying to death why I went away and forgot it without so much as a farewell sip?" he demanded indignantly, staggering into a snowdrift. "Whuff! You'll do well to be watching your step," he warned Ringgold, digging himself out and reeling forward again. "Faith, and there's a heavy ground swell rolling, and—whuff!"

Ringgold muttered every step of the frozen mile, but dared not abandon the fool Irishman in such weather. Patrick Flynn whuffed manfully over the last ground swell, and took fourteen seconds to turn stone sober.

There before them, under the weird wheel of the Northern Lights, a hulking shadow dragging two coal-oil cans came backing out of the blacksmith shop.

"Slater!" yelled Ringgold, and charged across the snow.

The frontier giant whirled to touch off a match and toss it into the interior. At once the blacksmith shop's door became the roaring mouth of a furnace, a torch to light up Slater's wolfish grin and the knife he yanked from his belt.

Beserk at the thought of damage to *Harvey's Hammer,* Ringgold bored in recklessly. Slater's first slash ripped his blanket coat to the ribs, but Ringgold chopped at Slater's knife arm and saw the blade spin away. He drove his fist into teeth, and Slater got up from the snow, spitting blood, and knocked Ringgold flat. He rolled from under Slater's wicked boots, regained his feet to slug at Slater's eyes.

Spilling across the snow toward the fire came canal gangs from the shanties, soldiers from Fort Brady, half-dressed citizens of Sault Ste. Marie. They saw jungle law under the North Star. "Him or me!" hollered Ringgold. "Give us room!"

A roof timber crashed in a shower of sparks. Flames licked out at a nearby toolshed and bathed the canal embankment that dropped sheer into the unfinished locks. In the background loomed the black spires of the pines.

With Ringgold's back to the roaring flames, Slater launched a full rush that sent them locked together through a wall of fire into the skeletonized building. Smelling of burnt hair and smouldering rags, they catapulted out another blazing wall into a snowbank.

They fought in savage silence, except for their labored breathing and the spat of bone against flesh. Reeling back from a blow between the eyes, Slater smashed into the toolshed. It toppled and burst under his weight, splashing tools across the snow.

Slater clawed at a double-bitted ax, and Ringgold snatched one for himself in the nick of time, but the odds switched heavily against him. "Meet a woodsman, sailor!" Slater snarled, and a sigh like the rustle of shrouds swept the crowd.

A moment later, the roof and all but one wall of the black-smith shop collapsed, burying Harvey's steam punch under roaring ruins. Not a head swerved from the duel with five-pound axes. The crowd saw expert against novice, lumber-jack against lakeman—and double-bladed death for the loser. Swift sparks flew as metal rang on metal. Slater struck and Ringgold parried. Ripped naked to the waist, wisps of smoke curling from their scorched pants, they fought across the snow. Slater handled his ax like a two-edged sword. His battered eyes and the greed that characterized him offered Ringgold a slender chance. The lakeman backed toward the embankment above the locks, into the shadows away from the fire. But, even in the uncertain light, Slater saw or sensed an opening. Ringgold blocked the vicious attack only to feel the blade sheared from his ax.

From the crowd came the keening "Ochone!" of Michael Phelan's widow.

Greedy for the kill, Slater stalked his victim, his damaged eyes set in a malignant squint. With only the ax handle for defense, Ringgold backed onto the embankment, counting each step he took. When he dared not take another, when he felt himself teetering on the sheer edge of uncertainty, he let the broken handle slip, then faked a desperate effort to pick it up.

Slater lunged forward with a whistling swing of steel, and, as Ringgold cat-leaped aside, Slater's murderous drive sent him off balance over the embankment. His scream split the night. Then his body thudded onto a limestone block in the murky depths twenty-five feet below.

He died within five minutes, but he took time to make his brag about killing Daniel Trowbridge to get his land partner's Wolverine Shares. With his last breath he cursed the canal.

With the clenched hands of a strong man who feels his helplessness, Ringgold stood rigid on the limestone floor of the canal locks, as if caught in evil spell. Only his bleak eyes moved—from Slater's broken body to the gaunt and haggard figure of another big man silhouetted up on the canal embankment against the feverish glow of a fire-flushed sky.

Tragic in his own despair, Ringgold looked up at Harvey, brought into sharp focus by the flaming ruins of a blacksmith shop that made a funeral pyre for *Harvey's Hammer*. In lake disasters the *Huron Bell's* skipper had seen lost causes embodied in men, but never such a stark picture of complete and utter failure.

BOOK FIVE

Superior Passport

And the last of all the figures
Was a heart within a circle,
Drawn within a magic circle;
And the image had this meaning:
"Naked lies your heart before me,
To your naked heart I whisper!"

Song of Hiawatha

BOOK FIVE

Superior Passport

1

WILDERNESS SEARCH

ON THE NIGHT that *Harvey's Hammer* roasted in the ruins of the blacksmith fire that Slater had died to set, the talking drums spoke from the wigwams at the foot of the rapids, and news rolled down the St. Mary's by wilderness telegraph at seventy-two pulse-beats a minute as relay stations from Church's Landing to the Narrows passed the word along to Potagannissing Bay on Drummond Island, where an Ojibway chief aroused Hyacinthe Beauharnais from sweet dreams of Susan Marie's Montreal grandmother.

At once the ancient *voyageur* hitched the sway-backed pony to his gaudy cutter and started for Sault Ste. Marie.

"Le premier jour de Mai, je donnerais a m'amie——"

He sang to the frosty March stars because Slater's confession of murdering Trowbridge made him free to swagger his sashes and plumes in public again, and moreover he felt a call. Had not the *Voices in the Rapids*, the *Mist People*, told him that he would be required at the Soo before his keg of *Napoleon* ran dry? And what now remained? No more than a swish and a gurgle, *voila tout!* So Hyacinthe Beauharnais followed his *Huntsmen* hunch and the legend on his cutter. That was no empty motto, *M'sieu —— Pret-a-Boyre!*

When he drew reign alongside the canal works, he found young Charles Harvey etched against the dawn, as stark and as stalwart as the chimney that stood out from the burned-down blacksmith shop. Driving an Irish gang to rescue the unfinished steam punch from under the smouldering timbers and hot ashes, the canal boss had rallied from the first shock of hopelessness to face the situation with Ringgold.

Marked by combat but quick to bounce back to his jaunty
self after the fatal fight with Slater, Captain Ringgold's rak-
ish grin double-dared the impossible. "We've lost time, sure,
maybe a month in one night, but we can build another blacksmith shop, skimp along with makeshift tools, and still meet
the May 19th deadline."

Harvey pointed out the gravest loss. "What about the battery of force bellows that went up in smoke? How can we
get the necessary replacements short of Saginaw and Detroit,
on the slow haul up the Snowshoe Pike? There's no time—"

"Hola!" cried a gay-sashed, plume-crowned *voyageur.*
"*C'est moi,* Hyacinthe Beauharnais, very much at your service, *mes cavaliers!*" What was required? Seven large forge
bellows? A *bagatelle!* Permit him the honor . . . .

Harvey banked on what the Soo called a wild-goose chase,
and Captain Ringgold went along for the ride of his life.
Down the St. Mary's on a shiny highway of ice zipped the
voyageur's cutter ballasted with kegs of rare *Napoleon* from
the Hudson's Bay Post.

Hoh! Hoh! Roulant my boule! Between songs a May-
hearted ancient put Gallic spice in his answers to Ringgold's
questions about Susan Marie. After her winter in Montreal,
would she return to the Soo as soon as navigation opened?
Who could doubt it, my friend, unless of course the *beaux
yeux* in her pretty head were turned in another direction by
some young gallant not so foolish as to call her his little sister—*Hoh! Hoh! Vole, mon coeur, vole!*

Out the mouth of the St. Mary's River and over the North
Channel onto Georgian Bay in Lake Huron crisped the cutter with Hyacinthe Beauharnais steering between Great Man-
itoulin Island and La Cloche Mountain toward the Canadian outposts that lighted lonely candles in the northern
nights: Owen Sound, Hurontario Mills, Nottawasaga, Tober-
moray, Penetanguishine; fish and fur stations, sawmill set-
tlements, places that had welcomed Champlain's scouts years

before the *Mayflower* sailed; places that laughed and turned
cartwheels at the familiar motto on the cutter: *Pret-a-Boyre!*

Hyacinthe Beauharnais knew his frontier. It was a long
winter. The *habitants* and *hivernants* liked to be convivial,
but, until the *voyageur* arrived, it had seemed ages before
the first boat of the new season would blow for a landing
with fresh supplies. At every stop the pattern became more
familiar. The Canadians pulled their noses, stroked their
chins thoughtfully, *Mais oui,* they would like to oblige
their old friend, but this was no small matter—to give up,
even at a fancy price, the only forge bellows in the village,
n'est-ce-pas?

Hyacinthe Beauharnais had one Napoleonic answer, *"Mes
amis"*—raising his glass—*"Pret-a-Boyre!"*

And Captain Ringgold offered the toast that closed each
deal. "To the Soo Canal—yours and ours—international
highway to a better world!"

After a nine-day absence the lake captain and the voyageur
returned to Saulte Ste. Marie. They had worn out countless
relays of rugged Canadian ponies; they had crossed an ice-
bound bay large enough to deserve the distinction as the
sixth Great Lake; they had dodged through islands as thick as
mice and skirted the largest freshwater island in the world,
they had covered hundreds of miles over the howling map of
March to deliver seven bellows to Harvey.

2

SHILLELAGHS AND KNUCKLE-DUSTERS

The canal boss hadn't been sitting on his hands. Already
smoke poured from the chimney of the new blacksmith shop,
and carpenters swarmed the length of the giant oak shaft.
From Pendrill's Sawmills near the mouth of the Tahquamenon River on Whitefish Bay in Lake Superior, John Tall-
man Whiting had bought, borrowed, or appropriated—the

old timer's attitude discouraged inquiry—one pair of forge bellows.

Now, combined with the *voyageur's* seven, Whiting's gift made a battery of eight forge bellows to warm the cockles of *Harvey's Hammer*. Fires were never banked, Sundays excepted. The furnaces roared around the clock to make up for lost time.

There were bristling changes along the cut. Harvey posted guards and nailed up warnings: NO TRESPASSING!——KEEP OUT!——TRESPASS AT YOUR PERIL!

In a speech at Town Meeting, Ringgold served blunt notice on all malcontents. "Anyone caught molesting canal property will be shot first and prosecuted second!"

The Irish canallers, spoiling for trouble, hefted their applewood shillelaghs; the canny Scots carried knuckle-dusters in their pockets. Every shanty gang was loaded for bear and ready to give a wildcat first bite.

But all anti-canal violence apparently had died with Cole Slater. The Wolverine Land Company disclaimed any connection with his arson. Fat Philo Worts and Doctor Musgrave, bulging with confidence, button-holed prospectors from Iron Bay and Copper Harbor, to pick out the land plums already reserved for the Canal Company by Harvey. In the *Soo Sentinel,* Jay Bisby hawked and spat at *Harvey's Hammer*. His headings were widely quoted by other sheets at the civilized end of the Snowshoe Pike:

> Michigan To Get Free Canal — Brash Upstart To Get Lesson — Public Demands That State Enforce Contract To Letter — 750,000 Acres of Timber and Choice Mineral Lands to be Thrown Open to Public Entry May 19th — Stampede to Upper Peninsula Looms at Open of Navigation — Canal Company Stock Drops Fifty Per Cent!

On the last Sunday in March, Captain Ringgold borrowed a sleigh to show Genesee Trowbridge the ice caves at the mouth of the Tahquamenon River on Whitefish Bay in Lake Superior. The wind whipped her pale cheeks alive, and the imp of nonsense in him made her laugh for the first time since Slater's boast about killing her father. Tragedy, he observed, had softened her into a more lovable young woman.

"When you smile," he said, "you're prettier than a mackinaw boat in a ten-mile breeze."

"No compliments, please!" A dimple showed. "If that wild little Indian of yours in Montreal overheard such a thing, she'd scratch my eyes out."

He sobered instantly. "Do you think she'll come back to me this spring?"

"I wish I were as sure of my own happiness as I am of yours," she said wistfully.

"Blast that Harvey!" Ringgold pretended annoyance. "Every time I take you out we devote the day to him."

"Why I haven't even mentioned his name."

"You don't need to. There's a full-sized picture of him in your eyes!"

"If it's that easy to see," Genesee said in a small voice, "why hasn't he paid some attention?"

"What can you expect in a country where it's ten months winter and two months poor sledding," Ringgold growled.

Early Monday morning he rammed into Canal Headquarters and talked turkey to his boss. "Whether you make your deadline or whether some fancy-pants engineers finish the job, the Soo Canal's wiped out the portage business. I figure the Canal Company ought to buy the Trowbridge outfit from Genesee for just what her father paid for it. I guess you could call it buying good will——"

"Good will?" Harvey reared back in his chair. "Whose good will?"

"Mine!" said Ringgold flatly.

Harvey shot him in a quick look, shuffled papers on his desk, smiled and held out his hand. "That's a bargain at any price," he said in dead earnest and added: "She's a good looking girl."

"Not mine!" Ringgold said.

"Who said she was?" Harvey came from behind the desk and studied his unshaven jaw in a cracked wall mirror. "You know, if and when I marry Lake Superior to the Lower Lakes and grab a little time for myself——"

Ringgold grinned. "I was beginning to wonder if you knew that about half the people in the world are supposed to get interested in the other half."

But Harvey still had a job to do. As March roared out, it was *Harvey's Hammer* against Lake Superior's rock ledge in a showdown that had only one month and nineteen days to go.

3

SPRING BREAKUP

In Detroit, the waterfront hotels were bursting at the buttons with land speculators.

In Buffalo, a chartered propeller kept steam up for distinguished passengers from New York and New England, while the Canal Company directors and their new engineers waited for the Upper Lakes to be declared open to navigation.

In Cambridge, a Harvard professor's sputtering quill finally reached the last line of his poem—*To the Land of the Hereafter!*—but, judging by the newspaper reports, there need be no hurry about sending Cousin Ringgold the verses, promised him before the first ship sailed through the canal.

In Montreal, a young girl—like a bouquet of arbutus peeping from her furs—saw the first sign of spring on a sleighride, but then her chin pushed out, round and smooth and firm as a darning egg, and she told her delighted escorts: "Me, I adore Montreal!"

Later, with her Beaufait cousins, Susan Marie visited the watchtower studio of Lord Dunbar. She shook her head and made a reproachful face at him as her finger traced dust on the base of his unfinished clay model of the Lakes.

The handsome nobleman shrugged carelessly. "I have had better things to do with my time." He pointed to his latest studies and impressions that thronged the room with a single personality. "These charcoals and watercolors of you are the finest work I've ever done."

Susan Marie paid a blush for the compliment. "You do me too much honor," she replied in the formal manner taught convent girls, but she could not help adding spitefully: "I know someone not so nice, who would never dream of giving up *his* precious Lakes for anything!"

Lord Dunbar winced at mention of this someone whom she claimed to detest but who never seemed far from her thoughts. However, with dogged British persistence, he continued the speech he had planned.

"I have been inspired by you all winter. I should like to hope that such inspiration might consent to remain with me all my life. May I dare ask whether——"

"Please, you promised!" Her finger scolded his lips, then she gave him a saying that was her way to answer any question that came unwelcome or too soon. "Me, I am deaf in that ear, my friend!"

He followed her to the window where they could see, far below, the blue ribbon of the St. Lawrence streaming between ice and snow as it carried the color of the five Great Lakes to the Atlantic.

Susan Marie broke a long silence. "Down there many years ago," she began, "I think more than half a century, my great-grandfather and another Irishman were riding in a North West Fur Company *bateau*. My great-grandfather was quite old and his countryman was quite young, but their hearts were the same age. They sang so much that they ran

out of songs and then, as the *voyageurs* rowed hard to reach
Montreal before darkness, they made up a song of their own,
my great-grandfather and his young friend who was homesick for Dublin."

"If you know it," Lord Dunbar begged, "I would like to
hear you sing this song of theirs."

"All the world does not give credit to my great-grandfather
for his part in making up the song," Susan Marie said, her
cheeks a little pink. "All the world gives credit only to
young Thomas Moore." Her eyes flashed. "But was not my
grandfather just as Irish, and are not all Irish born poets,
and could any Irishman in the same *bateau* with Tom
Moore keep from singing his own share of a new song?"

Lord Dunbar hastened to agree with her. "But please
sing it for me."

In a low voice, for his ears alone, never taking her gaze
from the blue rhythm of the St. Lawrence, Susan Marie sang
the Canadian Boat song:

> *Faintly as tolls the evening chime,*
> *Our voices keep tune and our oars keep time.*
> *Soon as the woods on shore look dim,*
> *We'll sing at St. Ann's our parting hymn.*
> *Row, brothers, row, the stream runs fast,*
> *The Rapids are near and the daylight's past.*

"It is a strange, haunting melody that beats to the flash and
dip of the *voyageurs'* oars," murmured Susan Marie "It is a
song that says, we must hurry, there is not much time left,
we may arrive too late—or not at all. It is a song that says,
we must move on into the darkness that lies ahead of all
voyageurs, so fill your eyes and your heart with what is here
now, fill them quickly, because we have no time to stay, and
because we will never pass this way again, you or I,—and,
even if we should, we would not be the same, and the place
itself would be changed."

Row, brothers, row, the stream runs fast,
The Rapids are near and the daylight's past.

Almost under her breath Susan Marie repeated the refrain. Both her eyes and her voice were troubled. "I am sorry. I don't understand why I have told you all this about the song of my great-grandfather and Thomas Moore."

"I'm afraid I understand," Lord Dunbar said. "Only too well." He went to his clay model and made a motion as if to sweep it to the floor.

Susan Marie caught his sleeve, and her mood completely changed. "If you think I mean to hurry back to Sault Ste. Marie, you are very far from understanding either a song or a girl. Oh, no! I am going to stay here in Montreal to see that you finish *your* Lakes. I care nothing for *his!*"

While she spoke, the Lakes were making themselves heard. Almost half a continent away, at Duluth, Minnesota Territory, the chinook blew and the ice-sheets cracked loose from the shores of Fond du Lac Bay.

Here came the spring breakup with the first salvo of artillery to rout winter. In thundering cannonades the warming winds shot ice floes out into Lake Superior. As always, the fiercest battle raged along the narrow channel of the St. Mary's River where juggernauts of ice jammed and jostled and refused safe passage to ships from Lake Huron until the second week in May. Meanwhile, spring floods closed the Snowshoe Pike, suspending all overland mail communications. For more than a month the outside world heard nothing from Sault Ste. Marie.

4

Showdown: Three-Ton Punch

Behind that white wall of silence, Harvey raced to meet his deadline, pinning his hopes on three tons of wood and

metal. Before April was a week old an Irish gang heaved
and grunted and hauled the business end of the steam punch
from the blacksmith shop. Harvey had built a drill to smash
a rock reef laid down by the Algonquin Glacier ages ago.
Wearing a smile wider than a slice of honeydew melon, he
invited the entire Wolverine Land Company to witness the
afternoon's event. They stood rooted on the pier when they
saw the size of the machine that had been fitted into the towering pile driver on the scow out in the ice-tossed water.

"Put your eyes back in your head for a rest!" yelled Captain Ringgold from the scow to Jay Bisby. "The show hasn't
even begun to commence!"

Harvey boomed orders and jumped into two dozen places
at once. He helped string guides into the frame of the
pile-driver; he fixed a system of ropes and pulleys to hitch his
punch to the drum of the steam engine operated by Patrick
Flynn; he checked the reels that worked ropes from the scow
to the opposite piers so the scow could be held steady or moved
by turning the reels; he marked a gauge on the thirty-foot
shaft of oak to show how deep the punch must be driven
through the rock reef.

"When the orange band slaps the water level, that's deep
enough——"

"Orange?" howled Patrick Flynn. "Any color but orange!"
He hauled out a bucket and brush to paint all Ireland. "Did
you say green, sir? Then green it shall be, and bad cess to
the Prince of Orange!"

Captain Ringgold stepped forward with a bottle, and a
voice that could be heard in Canada.

"With plain raspberry shrub, I christen you *Harvey's
Hammer!*" he told the steam punch, breaking the bottle across
its steel nose. "And you'd better be a teetotal success!"

The canal gangs whooped and hollered and hurled their hats. For a moment Harvey grinned like a schoolboy and waved to them, but then his muscles tightened into knots and his heart climbed into his throat so that his voice sounded thin as wire:

"Time for testing!"

Hushed as the white pines that overlooked the scene, the crowd watched. The great white oak shaft poised above the water, a mighty finger of fate pointed from a foreboding sky. Then the steam engine pulsed, guide wires sang, and the reels worked the scow into position.

"Move her a hair!" Harvey roared. "Move her a split *red* hair!" The scow shifted over the reef. Float ice made calculations uncertain, but Harvey's hand flashed the signal. "Let her go!"

Down drove the drillhead, down slammed the shaft. Plang! Wham! Whuck! Plunge! Strike! Hoist! *Harvey's Hammer* reared up and smashed down until the shamrock green on her shaft slapped the water level.

"She works!" Ringgold breathed to Harvey, low as a prayer, and then the canal gangs tore the roof from the world with their cheers.

From that moment, three crews working eight hours each, kept *Harvey's Hammer* in constant motion—except Sundays. Night and day, rain or shine or whatever, three tons of fist on a thirty-foot arm smashed through the thin edge of reef at the Lake Superior entrance and advanced toward the hard hump of the ledge nearer the coffer dam.

While *Harvey's Hammer* fought to eliminate more than thirty thousand square yards of obstruction before May 19th, another necessary milestone was reached.

One April morning, Michael Phelan's widow, hanging out a wash of Keweenaw nips for her shanty-boys, shaded her eyes and saints-be-praised the sight as construction mules, lowered for duty long months ago, were hoisted out of the cut to signal completion of the locks. That same afternoon the bonny widow stood rosy-cheeked and proud-eyed with her three small daughters as young Harvey opened the sluice gates of the cofferdam and let Lake Superior into the finished canal prism in a moving mile of water.

Faith, and could a poor woman be blamed for thinking that maybe a wee bit of the credit belonged to herself? Faith, and indeed she could not, replied three brisk nods and three pairs of snapping blue eyes so like her own, for it was naught but true, and divil a man could deny it!

Who cared to deny it? Who dared? "Three cheers for Mrs. Phelan!" bellowed Patrick Flynn, love bulging his chest. "Three cheers for the one that looks like an angel and cooks like an angel!"

The widow blushed prettier than a peony as the canal gangs tried to throw their hearts—not just their hats—into the air. But *Harvey's Hammer* sounded above the hurrahs. The steam engine on the scow rumbled May-nineteen, May-nineteen, May-nineteen. Harvey cocked an ear to the warning. Hands and jaws clenched, he stood by the sluice gates and watched the silver highway pave Michigan's Mighty Mile, the most important mile on earth. Then he stabbed a glance toward the rock reef, and a blue vein writhed on his forehead.

Plang! Wham! Whuck! Plunge! Strike! Hoist! The days flew across N. Currier's calendar. *Harvey's Hammer* advanced on a front one hundred feet wide against an enemy one hundred yards long. May-nineteen, May-nineteen, May-nineteen! The steam punch raced time over a rock reef.

The first great test came when the ledge hump showed below. While Patrick Flynn nursed the steam engine, with Harvey and Nichols working the reels, Ringgold maneuvered the scow over three feet of solid rock.

"If she can beat her way through what's below," said Ringgold, peering into the depths, "then she can smash through
the earth and bust out of the Great Wall of China!"

Harvey's Hammer thundered into motion. Plang! Wham!
Whuck! The shamrock gauge on the great oak shaft stopped
two feet above water level. Plunge! Strike! Hoist! The gauge
showed one foot to go. Plang! Wham! Whuck!

"The only color!" bragged Patrick Flynn, as the green gauge
slapped water.

Around the clock the steam punch battered into Lake
Superior's reef. She wore thin from her three tons, and as
she lost weight she gained scars, but she drove and drilled
through the thickest sections of rock. *Harvey's Hammer* had
the soul of her namesake: there was no stopping her, short
of destruction.

The most decisive test arrived the last week in April. Young
Harvey had delayed the showdown, now he had to know.
His steam punch could smash a rock reef, but the vital question remained: Was it breaking the reef into small enough
chunks for a dredge to remove it?

He sat on the pier—sat because his knees were knocking—
and waited for the verdict. Captain Ringgold operated the
levers on the Osgood dredge, and Patrick Flynn wheedled the
engine. The scoop dipped water, scraped, emerged dripping
—and empty. Four times it failed, until Harvey jumped to
his feet.

"Put on all the power you've got!" he exploded. "Bring up
that rock or bust the dredge to blazes!" The Irish gangs
blinked and nudged one another and stared at their two-fisted
boss.

Captain Ringgold, tense as a trap, fussed with levers. He
drew back the scoop to its limit, scraped bottom, then applied
the last reserve of holding power. Squealing and trembling,
the dredge almost shook to pieces. Slowly the scoop ap-

proached the surface. It came out of water, full to the brim
with broken stone, and not a lump of it as large as a man's
hand.

"Peanuts!" hollered Ringgold. "Peanuts for Barnum's
elephants!" And all the canallers whooped at the broken stone
and took up the delirious chant.

5

VOTE OF CONFIDENCE

Two weeks later, on May 10th, 1855, the St. Mary's River,
in one of the latest seasons on record, finally opened to navigation, and the ships that had been waiting out in Lake
Huron went fullsteam toward the Soo, their decks mobbed
with land speculators hurrying to file claims on the iron and
copper locations that the Canal Company would forfeit for
failure to meet its deadline within the next nine days.

In the main salon of the lead steamer, the canal directors
—along with McAlpine and Clark, their new-hired team of
famous engineers—traded glum looks across a solemn table.
President Corning of the New York Central Railroad, Brooks
of the Michigan Central, Erastus Fairbanks of the Vermont
Scales Factory, these were not men to nurse false hopes.
True, the State of Michigan had reached no final decision on
their request for a time extension, but the political pressure
being brought to bear against them by the Land Lobby in
Lansing was overwhelming. At best, the directors anticipated
a prolonged legal struggle, with the binding terms of the contract dead against them.

"Unless Harvey's gone ahead and rigged up something that
would——" Erastus Fairbanks coughed in embarrassment
and looked an apology at the famous engineers. "You still
don't think it's possible?"

McAlpine and Clark shook their heads, peered down their
noses at him.

"I expect you're right," sighed Erastus Fairbanks, "and I hate to keep harping on it, but our Mr. Morse and brother Thad had an idea that——"

"Morse!" President Corning snorted. "The way you three Fairbanks brothers talk about that Morse youngster, a person might reckon he was one of the partners in the business!"

"Well, he's a St. Johnsbury boy with a level head on his shoulders, comes of good stock and is quick with figures. We aren't showing him any favors he hasn't earned, but Thad seems to think he might work himself all the way up the ladder to the top of the Company some day. Thad says——"

"Thad thinks, Thad says! The President of the New York Central stirred irritably. "I'm tired of hearing what that day-dreaming brother of yours thinks and says!"

The President of Fairbanks Scales gave a sympathetic nod. "I know what you mean. My brother Joe and I get to feeling the same way every once in a while. It wouldn't be so hard if we could point to a lot of mistakes and blame him for them, but Thad's so confounded right most of the time!"

"Just answer me this: What does Thaddeus know about canals?"

"Nothing, nothing at all," admitted Erastus Fairbanks "But Thad didn't know boo about platform scales either," he added mildly. "Not until he went ahead and invented them——"

6

ARGUING THE RIGHT OF FIRST PASSAGE

Charles Harvey, poker-faced, met the steamer and welcomed the directors onto McKnight's Dock at the end of navigation below the rapids. "Carriages are ready to take us to the rock reef, gentlemen!" he called. "I most earnestly solicit your opinions," he told the imported engineers who already looked upon him as a subordinate. "Very anxious to see your reaction——"

Jouncing buggies carried them along the water-gleaming mile of canal to the Lake Superior entrance. McAlpine and Clark started to pile out onto the pier to inspect the submerged construction.

"Don't exert yourselves," said Harvey blandly. "I've arranged for us to view it quite comfortably from here." He pointed to the hills of broken stone rising from the opposite bank, then he crowed: "There's your rock reef!"

They stared and, as the miracle dawned on them, jumped out of their shoes to overwhelm Harvey with praise. But it remained for Erastus Fairbanks to pay the highest tribute to the young man he and his brothers had hired originally as a traveling salesman.

"Brother Thad would admire to see this," he beamed. "Even Thad couldn't have invented himself out of trouble any better."

Riding high on compliments, Harvey showed them his steam punch still pounding away, trimming the edges of the channel. They stood thunderstruck while *Harvey's Hammer* sledged blows of more than thirty tons to the square inch on rock twelve feet below the surface.

McAlpine and Clark hung on Harvey's every word. It was yes, Mr. Harvey, yes, indeed, sir, and it was Charles T. Harvey, Boss of the Works!

In Sault Ste. Marie the boatloads of land speculators heard disquieting dock-side rumors and swarmed toward the *Soo Sentinel.* Even when sour-faced Jay Bisby told them the news, they couldn't get it through their heads. "But what happened?" they demanded. "What happened?"

Captain Ringgold swaggered up Water Street with the answer. "Harvey happened, you vultures! I trust you all have return passages!"

He delighted in baiting the long-faced opportunists. "Lord Byron's poetic comment on gambling is very much to the point. *In play there are two pleasures for your choosing: the one is winning, and the other is losing.* You boys have had the *other* pleasure! So long, *losers!*"

Overnight the Wolverine Land Company dissolved. Philo Worts and Doctor Musgrave skipped the Soo, leaving nothing but bad debts behind. Jay Bisby sold out to an honest publisher and vanished.

But every day the Soo bustled and bulged with more arrivals from below. Government inspectors and state engineers swarmed along the canal to check the two great locks and the waterway that bypassed the rapids. Celebrities spilled into town from every boat as Governor Bingham sent out calls for Michigan's favorite sons—the Iron Hunters, Trail Blazers, Legend Makers, who had earned the historic honor of berths aboard the first ship to sail from the Lower Lakes into Lake Superior.

Every ship owner and captain on the lakes—from Montreal to Milwaukee—fought for the privilege of taking his boat through as the lead vessel. Sail argued with steam for the right of first passage. There were riots at every port of call on the inland seas.

At the Soo, young Charles Harvey and Patrick Flynn led the fight for the *Huron Belle*—Captain Eureka Longfellow Ringgold, Master. Harvey pulled political strings; Flynn used persuasion of another kind.

"So, it's that old tub of yours you'd be favoring over the *Huron Belle,* is it?" he growled to a three-hundred-pound Swede between six and seven feet tall. "Ah, well, it's a free world," said Patrick Flynn, polishing his fist, "so if you want it, you'll get it, but what about your poor old mother when you're gone?"

As the parade of paddle wheels, propellers, and windjammers beelined for the Soo, Captain Ringgold met every boat

that docked below the rapids. He stared his eyes out down
the St. Mary's River. He waited in vain for Susan Marie's
return.

Those were the days when he took the habit of listening
to the *Voices of the Rapids*. At first he heard nothing but the
roar and rumble and swish-swash of the water, but as his
loneliness lengthened, he began to distinguish a few words
the *Huntsmen* spoke. He remembered what Susan Marie
had told him about the brigade of *Mist People*, forever digging their paddles toward Lake Superior. . . .

For Ringgold they had one song and nothing more:

> *Long ships passing, speak to my love.*
> *Long ships passing, bring my love to me.*

Over and over the *Huntsmen* sang that song under the
sound and fury of the rapids. Hyacinthe Beauharnais nodded understandingly when told about it. "A man hears only
the echo of his heart," but he shook his head when asked what
possible reason could be keeping Susan Marie in Montreal.
"A reason?" he shrugged. "My friend, she is a woman, *voila
tout!*"

Michael Phelan's widow offered Ringgold scant comfort.
"Sure, and it's high time you woke to your senses!" she sniffed,
setting pies out to cool. "Little Sister, indeed!"

Her eyes snapped. "If it was me, mind you, standing in her
shoes, with naught but mimories of 'Little Sister' in my ear,
I'd keep you on tacks another month of Sundays, if I *iver*
decided to favor you with my presence!"

Then the widow gave Ringgold a smack and a squeeze
until her cheeks glowed like a cranberry bog. "But, ninny-
hammer that you are, it's wishing you all the luck of the Irish,
I am!"

Less than a week before the date set for the first ship to
enter the Soo Canal, Charles Harvey called Captain Ringgold
to Elmwood and made a ceremony of pouring two glasses of

raspberry shrub. He broke his good news in a toast: "To the *Huron Belle!* First to sail into Lake Superior!"

Stubbornness carved Ringgold's lips. "Not without Susan Marie aboard."

Harvey hit the ceiling with a roar. "For a lovesick whim you'd throw away the greatest honor these lakes will ever see?" His eyes measured Ringgold. "Yes you would!" he said simmering. "Okay, I'll hold the *Illinois* in reserve as second choice. We'll wait for your precious Miss Johnston!"

Next morning he ordered both boats decked out with bunting and banners, dolled up for the wedding of the lakes.

7

Mr. Longfellow's Compliments to the Soo Canal

In the afternoon a letter and a package arrived for Captain Ringgold from Cambridge, Massachusetts. The letter said:

> DEAR COUSIN: Herewith please find one poem requested three years ago this month. The size of the product exceeds by far the few verses in Horace Greeley style ordered to boom your beloved lake, but I trust the contents are satisfactory. In fairness to my speed as a craftsman, I must state that my Lake Superior poem was completed in advance of Mr. Harvey's Lake Superior canal, and I insist on recording the fact that you heckled us both into our respective chores in June, 1852. . . .
>
> Seriously, cousin, this Indian Edda is founded on the tradition of a hero sent among them to clear their rivers, forests, and fishing-grounds. Different tribes knew him as Manabozho, Tarenyawagon, or Hiawatha. . . .

Reverently, Captain Eureka Longfellow Ringgold picked up the *Song of Hiawatha*. His eyes daydreamed across the manuscript pages recognizing familiar landmarks—Escanaba, Tahquamenaw—a whole Empire and a Nation springing

alive, flowing across paper in the rise and fall and repetition
of Ojibway music, of Lake Superior's pulse.

The troubadour in Captain Ringgold appreciated that his
hands held a literary landmark every bit as unique as the Soo
Canal's place among the waterways. America's best-known
poet had written his best-known poem but, as Ringgold read
the wild sweet notes in his cabin aboard the *Huron Belle*, he
realized he needed someone special to share the magic with
him, to learn it by heart with him. He pressed apple blos-
soms on the page that said: "O my sweetheart, my Algonquin!" and he readdressed the package to Susan Marie Beaufait Eldridge Johnston, Montreal.

8

WEDDING OF THE LAKES

Two days after Charles Harvey celebrated his twenty-sixth
birthday, Governor Bingham, in a tall-hatted ceremony alongside the locks, accepted the Soo Canal on behalf of his state
in consideration of seven hundred and fifty thousand acres
of timber and mineral lands in Michigan's Upper and Lower
Peninsula.

"In spite of cholera, sub-zero weather, malicious connivers,
the isolation of an outpost frozen away from civilization six
months of the year, and other hardships and handicaps beyond our imagination," stated Governor Bingham handsome-
ly, "the management working in the public interest and for
the future, insisted—not in merely meeting its obligations—
but in going beyond the specifications required. To the best
of my knowledge, this has been the most honorably per-
formed contract ever entered into with a state or national
government——"

Erastus Fairbanks spoke for the St. Mary's Falls Ship
Canal Company. He revealed that the locks and gates were

the largest ever made, that the engineering features were without precedent in American history, and that the job had cost the contractors more than double the original estimate.

"We never figured on skimping," he said. "Skimpers don't get along in a country where there's free competition. We put the best we've got into everything we produce, whether it's scales or railroads or canals. If we didn't, companies that offered better products would drive us out of business. My partners and I stand for private enterprise and the profit system because we believe it operates for the public welfare."

The scalemaker's Vermont honesty drove any pompous touch from the proceedings. "And we're counting on Mr. Harvey's selections of pine and iron and copper lands to yield us reasonable returns for our investment risk in constructing Michigan's Mighty Mile——"

Harvey's broad-shouldered figure dominated the speaker's stand as he had dominated the canal works, from the day Captain Ringgold had put the bug in his ear to this hour of triumph. "No need making speeches," he told them curtly. "If we've done a good job, the Soo Canal will do the talking for us." He faced toward Lake Superior and cupped his hands for a shout that rolled like thunder over water.

"Gangway!" he hollered. "Gangway for tomorrow!"

Steamboat whistles blew and mission bells rang out the news that Charles T. Harvey, a traveling salesman for the Fairbanks Scales Company of St. Johnsbury, Vermont, a young fellow sent to Sault Ste. Marie for a rest cure, had promoted a canal on the roof of the world at the edge of nowhere, and then had gone on to build it in less than two years since breaking ground.

"And him that never put up so much as a white picket fence before!" muttered Patrick Flynn to Michael Phelan's widow, shaking his head in bafflement. "Him that doesn't drink, doesn't smoke, doesn't swear, doesn't play cards, doesn't break the Sabbath and, for all I know, doesn't even—"

Patrick Flynn stopped with an Ouch! and rubbed his arm. "Sure, and every word I had in my mouth," he continued with injured dignity, "was that, for all I know, he doesn't even dream about doing such things." His smile came out broad as his brogue. "Ah, pinch me again, Mrs. Phelan," he said, "for whether it's waking or dreaming I am when your sweet self's around, is more than my poor wits can tell!"

The crowning event of the gala day was put in motion as Harvey strode to McKnight's dock. There his belongings lay piled, for he had vacated Elmwood and was headed west with half the Soo hitching their wagons to his star. At the last minute he talked to Captain Ringgold, gripped his hand regretfully, and ordered all baggage put aboard the steamer *Illinois,* Captain Jack Wilson, Master.

Celebrities thronged across the gangplank onto the vessel that, second only to the *Huron Belle,* had played the leading role in building the Soo Canal. From ashore Ringgold separated the titans from the small fry of flag-wavers and moneybags.

Legend Maker Schoolcraft couldn't come, but Iron Hunter Burt and Trail Blazer Cass were on hand: Old Bill Burt who had discovered every iron range in the Lake Superior jack pot clear to the mighty Mesaba in Minnesota Territory; seventy-year-old Senator Cass who had explored and adventured across this wilderness of waterways in a paddle-and-portage birchbark canoe.

Next to Burt and Cass on the after-deck of the *Illinois* stood Peter White and Charles Harvey, a pair of young giants to balance the old titans: Peter White, already on his way toward making the region around Marquette known as Peter White's country; Charles Harvey who had nowhere to go because he had already reached the highwater mark of a lifetime. Charles Harvey, destined, among other feats, to build the first elevated railroad in New York City, but Charles Harvey leaving behind at the age of twenty-six a work that no man, not even himself, could surpass.

For those who could listen, the *Voices of the Rapids* were singing a song that would hold true for a hundred years to come. Invisible behind the smoke of foam and spray, the *Huntsmen,* the *Mist People,* everlastingly rode their canoes out in midstream and sang the glory of the Soo Canal:

Greater than the Suez, greater than the Panama, greater than the Suez and the Panama Canals combined . . . .

With a toot to be heard in the next century, the *Illinois* pulled away from the river dock below the rapids and entered the Soo Canal. As the locks lifted her up, Captain Ringgold watched from the pier, his face long and tight. Michael Phelan's widow waved from the deck with Patrick Flynn's handkerchief while the brawny Irishman beside her held a bouquet of three small daughters. At a little distance on the same deck, Genesee Trowbridge twirled a green parasol and pretended not to be looking at Harvey. From up above on the top deck, Captain Wilson shook a megaphone at Ringgold and called:

"All aboard for Iron Bay, Marquette, Copper Harbor, Eagle River, Ontonagon, Isle Royale, Apostle Islands, Fond du Lac, Duluth, Superior City, North Star, and Setting Sun!"

Flags flying, a German band playing, the steamer *Illinois* locked-up toward Lake Superior, taking Charles T. Harvey across the rim of the horizon.

9

Gangway For Tomorrow

Captain Ringgold kept his vigil. He waited while the steamer *Baltimore,* Captain John Reed, Master, passed through the locks, bound eastward. He saw the brig *Freeman* become the first sail vessel on the canal, bound up. He recognized history on the hustle as the brigantine *Columbia* came winging out of Lake Superior to drop her sails while the locks took her down below the Falls of St. Mary's; the *Columbia*, Captain Judson Wells, Master, with a hundred tons of Cleveland-Cliffs iron ore on her decks, the first cargo from Lake Superior's mines, first in a series to turn the United States from a fifth-rate power into Number One among the nations.

Then, quite unexpectedly and unaccountably, Ringgold felt a small hand tucked into his large paw and there, perking up at him from under a bonnet all bows and buds, was his wild Irish Indian French Canadian American girl with eyes like rainbows struck by lightning, like the sunburst rapids of Sault Ste. Marie—his own Susan Marie.

"Miss me?" she asked. "Me, I came as soon as I heard the *Huntsmen* sing: *Long ships passing, speak to my love. Long ships passing, bring my love to me.*"

She carried *The Song of Hiawatha* under her arm, and she wore a dress to attract humming-birds and honey-bees. Had the *Huntsmen* really spoken to her from Lachine Rapids or had Hyacinthe Beauharnais sent word by wilderness telegraph? Or had Longfellow's poem brought her back? It made no difference to Ringgold. He had her in his arms, and that was all that mattered.

Reverend MacDougall. In scarlet sash and heron plumes, he gave the bride away and was best man for the groom.

The *Huron Belle,* with Ringgold at the wheel and Susan Marie in the crook of his arm for safekeeping, took a turn up the St. Mary's to cruise past Elmwood where Hiawatha, in a

They were married within the hour, Hyacinthe Beauharnais insisting on acting in a double role that confused the manner of speaking, had been born. Then the steamer side-wheeled into the canal and entered the locks.

Down below in the engine room, Hyacinthe Beauharnais began an old voyageur's game with lobsterish Angus Laing. Under the gimlet-eyed scrutiny of the dour Scot he placed three moccasins and a small stone on a drumhead of Algoma cheese. The object of the pastime, he explained, was for him to try to hide the stone so that no one could guess under which moccasin it reposed. Of course, his fingers were stiff as any blind man could see, but he might risk a wager merely to keep the interest alive.

"A poond!" called Angus Laing. "Put up or shut up, ye pea-souper!"

Hyacinthe Beauharnais sighed tolerantly, and the old *voyageur* game went its usual course. . . .

In the wheelhouse, Captain Ringgold and Susan Marie faced the future together with *The Song of Hiawatha* for a wedding present as the *Huron Belle* locked-up through the Soo Canal, the Northwest Passage, the key to empire, the national pike to Manifest Destiny. The steamer side-wheeled toward the iron-throned, copper-crowned Queen of Lakes, the great sweetwater sea, the lake with the name that showed how far she surpassed all other lakes—Lake Superior!

Ringgold kissed his bride. They were moving into Hiawathaland where the Pictured Rocks were murals painted by the past on the rocky headlands of the future. "Gangway!" said Ringgold softly. "Gangway for tomorrow!"

The *Huron Belle* blew for passage into Gitche Gumee, shining Big-Sea-Water.

Epilogue

Westward, westward Hiawatha
Sailed into the fiery sunset,
Sailed into the dusk of evening.

* * *

To the Land of the Hereafter!

Song of Hiawatha

Epilogue

MARKER FOR ALL TIME

In 1905, Charles T. Harvey, C. E., returned to Sault Ste. Marie to attend the Semicentennial Celebration held the first week in August. There were speeches and trips through the locks. Bands played all day and fireworks blazed all night. Indian souvenirs were sold in booths that stood where tepees once had been pitched. Forty thousand people came to pay tribute to the canal a young traveling salesman had completed fifty years in the past.

A handsome man, still vigorous in his seventies, Harvey rode a prancing white horse at the head of the parade that marched through gala streets where formerly the portage railroads had snaked along and sailing ships had been hauled by land around the rapids. As the Grand Marshal of the Semi-centennial, Harvey as usual was still leading the way. Behind him in their bunting-decked carriage trailed the dignitaries, including the Governor of Michigan and the Vice-President of the United States, the Speaker of the Senate and the Solicitor-General of the Dominion of Canada.

In the half century he had been away, Harvey had reason to be proud of such accomplishments as combining links of railroads into a chain stretched from Lake Superior to the Gulf of Mexico, acting as advisor to the Panama Canal Commission, and originating New York City's elevated railroad system, the Rapid Transit. But he had come back to the days of his youth, to his first and greatest achievement. Of all the works of man, the Soo Canal had no rival in importance, and its destiny was to grow more important with the years.

When plans were begun for the Centennial Celebration of 1955, the young General Agent of the St. Mary's Falls Ship Canal Company and the white-bearded Grand Marshal of the Semi-centennial belonged to history. Harvey's original locks, once derided as too large, long since had yielded in size to the Weitzel, the Poe, the Davis, the Sabin, and finally the tremendous MacArthur lock geared to the projected St. Lawrence Seaway—from the Soo, and from beyond the Soo, down the Great Lakes and their connecting waters to the Atlantic Ocean.

Now celebrating its hundredth birthday, Harvey's canal remained in the atomic era what it had been from the start— Gangway For Tomorrow! Soldiers from old Fort Brady guarded the locks and jet planes from nearby Kinross Air Base patrolled the skies above America's priceless mile. Only a few miles to the South, where once the Ojibway mailman had shuffled down the Snowshoe Pike toward civilization, the longest and costliest bridge in the world was being built to span the Straits of Mackinac and bring the Soo and Lake Superior immeasurably closer to the United States that moves on wheels.

But Harvey had paved the way. Every prospector who carried a Geiger counter in hopes of striking uranium beyond the Soo, every ship that passed through the locks laden with Superior iron for Lower Lakes steelmakers or prairie grain to feed the world, owed a tribute to Charles T. Harvey, the same tribute he himself had paid the canal-gang victims of the cholera epidemic: "Their marker is the Soo Canal."

Harvey now shares that marker with all the others who have made it possible, then and since—a monument indeed mightier than the pyramids — SOO CANAL!